HIGHLAND
REGIONAL
LIBRARY

WITHDRAWN

J. BASKWILL
16 GEARY
WATERNISH
ISLE OF SKYE IV55 8GQ

London Fields

By the same author

TYRO

LONDON FIELDS

by

John Milne

HIGHLAND
REGIONAL
LIBRARY

83 42285

Hamish Hamilton London

First published in Great Britain 1983
by Hamish Hamilton Ltd
Garden House 57–59 Long Acre London WC2E 9JZ

Copyright © 1983 by John Milne

British Library Cataloguing in Publication Data
Milne, John
  London fields.
  I. Title
  823'.914[F]   PR6063.I/

ISBN 0-241-10980-9

Photoset by Rowland Phototypesetting Ltd
Bury St Edmunds, Suffolk
Printed in Great Britain by
St Edmundsbury Press
Bury St Edmunds, Suffolk

'When a man denominates another his *enemy*, his *rival*, his *antagonist*, his *adversary*, he is understood to speak the language of self-love, and to express sentiments, peculiar to himself, and arising from his particular circumstances and situation. But when he bestows on any man the epithets of *vicious* or *odious* or *depraved*, he then speaks another language, and expresses sentiments, in which he expects all his audience are to concur with him. He must here, therefore, depart from his private and particular situation, and must choose a point of view, common to him with others; he must move some universal principle of the human frame, and touch a string to which all of mankind have an accord and symphony.'

David Hume, *An Inquiry concerning the Principles of Morals*: IX, Part 1.

For Sandra Milne

In Wandsworth

Chapter One

'I used to hate me titfer, the bugger.'
  'Titfer?'
  'Titfer tat . . . hat.'
  'And don't swear, it's not necessary.'
  'Sorry, sir. I didn't mean.'
  'Just go on.'
  'Okay . . . well I hated it. Me 'at. All the kids at our school never wore theirs and though my family were never any posher than anyone else I still had to always wear me 'at and me worsted short grey trousers, the buggers . . . sorry.'
  'Just go on.'
  'The trousers. They scratched me thighs and froze the knees. I had to wear them even in the winter, when the other kids wore jeans because their mothers made a fuss. My mother never made a fuss, she didn't want no trouble, and I didn't get to wear no jeans, nor dungarees, which is what we called them then . . . is all this off the subject?'
  'No. It's a start. School's as good a place as any for a start.'
  'Yes sir. I seemed to be frightened all the time at the first school. I preferred home. I still do. Well, ha! anyone would do here, wouldn't they?'
  There was no reply.
  'We had a portable radio in our house and my Grandad could get foreign stations on it, even though no one had any bleedin' idea what was being said. I might have been wrong sir.'
  'Why?'
  'I might have got the radios mixed up. I don't think we had a portable till quite a bit later . . . anyway, by the time I went to school we had got a portablenotnot.'

'A what?'

'Joke. Joke sir. We'd got a telly that was without a doubt definitely not portable. Definitely not.'

He paused but the man continued to write, and said, without looking up, 'Carry on. You mustn't keep stopping.'

'Okay. Our house was cosy all right. Each part of it had its own different feel, *smell* even, so that each part was private to you when you were in it. I could sit on the floor and be private in my own private place, even with my Mum and Dad there and even with my Grandad in hot pursuit of Alouise. I had to keep my knees off the oilcloth so I didn't get moaned at about catching cold but as long as I did that, as long as I sat there and followed the rules, didn't lie out of line with the pattern on the carpet or something, everything was all right. Nothing could go wrong. It was my place . . . *my* place my own . . . own. That's stupid, isn't it, sir? You don't know about "own" in our sense when you're little . . . but still it's true. Inside was mine but outside was the world and there's no control there at all.'

The listener was surprised at this, though he took great care not to allow the surprise to register on his face. He made a note on his pad.

'I knew it even then, you see. I'm not just making it up for now. For you . . . outside was old men who'd shout at you for riding your bike on the pavement and coppers who'd shout at you for not riding on the pavement. I remember, ha! one swept at me with his cape as I was going past: "Gercha! Git backin that yard!"'

He half stood from his seat as he quoted the supposed policeman, holding his clenched fist forward, as if he were clutching the cape. The listener looked, judging whether he should react, then motioned his subject back to his seat.

'It was years before I realized he could have caught me if he'd wanted.' He shook his head. 'Ha! I couldn't now imagine a copper of that generation running . . . could you, sir?'

There was no response. The listener was busy writing. Under 'Believes that the outside world lacks discipline' he wrote 'Has nostalgic wish for an old order. Policemen. Family'. The listener hesitated for a second, then drew a large question mark so that it was beside both sentences. It referred to both. The subject saw the mark, though he could not make out the writing to which it referred.

'Is it all right, sir?'

'Yes. Yes, everything is good. Fine. Carry on.'

'Just here. Just this about when I was little?'

That's just fine.'

'Okay then . . . the copper convinced me, when I was little, and that was the important bit, I suppose . . . I suppose just. Suppose.'

And he paused again as if the matter of supposition was of very great weight. He started again suddenly, almost catching his listener unawares.

'Anyway he was outside and I suppose that's what you want to hear. *Outside* was having to leg it through the arches when the trains went over and made that noise they make, God I hate that noise even now.' He smiled. 'Not that I come into contact with it much.'

'Outside is important, isn't it?'

I don't know. I really don't. All the dough they pay these prats all to tell a bloke in the jug that being outside is important. I know it's important, john, dunni? I'm not going home tonight like you. . . . *Am I*! These last words screamed out within him and his spine tensed and closed with his gut muscles.

He simply said, 'Yes,' and remembered to add again, 'sir.'

The man's eyes said he wanted more of this stuff so the subject continued: 'Outside was cold and grey and ugly and I never wanted to be there. I only wanted to be inside during that time.'

'With your mother?'

'What?'

'You wanted to be inside with your mother?'

'Course. She lived there.' You're not getting me at that, clever cods.

The listener wrote down that the speaker wanted to be inside with his mother when he was small, though he did not add any question mark.

'I didn't know anybody outside.' Don't you understand? 'Except that I had one friend, a boy in the next block, and there was always the Indian. The boy in the next block had a red pedal car but his Mum bought a house and they moved away. She had wax fruit and a telly that had doors and had to warm up. They kept a blue parrot. I remember the Indian better. He was the only . . .'

The subject checked himself. He was very far from having any prejudice towards black men, but there was no way of making the listener understand this quickly. He chose the polite form.

'He was the first coloured I'd ever seen, sir. He kept a tray that I wasn't tall enough to see into and he shouted something like, "Yeerwhal! Yeerwhal!" and he didn't seem to mind if I stared, though he would never talk to me. I dunno if he could talk English at all. He wore thin white trousers, even in the winter and we never bought any whatever-they-weres. I just never used to think the yard was "outside" in that hard way while he was there. That's what I've been trying to tell you.'

'Thank you.'

The subject looked carefully at the man's hands but he wrote nothing.

'The most outside place of all was the schoolyard,' he offered, as if to help the man.

'Tell me.'

'Oh . . . well. I didn't like it there at all. Everyone had to stand in their place on the first whistle and rush to get to a certain spot on the second and I never knew which line to be in or what spot to stand on. They all laughed and when I never knew where to go the teachers were kind, even when I couldn't find my coat the first few times. After that they just got my Mum in from the gate to fetch it.'

'You felt threatened?'

'Yes. All the kids had friends in the schoolyard and I didn't. Not then.'

'Did you later?'

'Yes . . . shall I tell you about them?'

'If you want . . . let's stick with this for now, eh? Were you about to say something else?'

'Yes but it's not important.'

The two men sat silent for a few seconds, closed together in the little barred room. Outside the sun escaped its cloudkeeper, as if to emphasise the 'important', as if it too would be moved to express some part of the subject's tale. Yes, the sun is there too, thought the subject, though it is not always there and he was sure would not be there for ever. This hurt him, an unexpected wounding that cut to him quickly and none too cleanly, as if 'for ever' were a real term, like 'life' or 'fifteen years', and these are, of course, the same thing. But now he saw the sun was neutral, touching the glass and the dirt that filtered it equally, lighting all before it without favour – though in its serenity it had lit the bars outside the window too; an oversight, surely. He squeezed his eyes against the sun's rays, and realized that the listener had been speaking.

'Sorry?'

'I said . . .'

The listener swung in his chair, so that he could see for himself whatever it was that had grasped his subject's attention outside the window. There was nothing to see; just the cell block beyond and the window near to, and far far off the sun burning his eyes in its winter whiteness and lowness. The listener stood and lowered the blind a little, so that there should be no harsh shadows cast onto his writing pad. It's *so* difficult to write against a shadow. He picked up the pen again and wrote 'Short attention span'.

'I said,' turning the pad face down, 'that we do have time for everything. There is no rush. But it *is* necessary to concentrate.'

'Does what I say help?'

'It helps me, yes.'

'But it all seems so far off the subject. How are you able to judge?'

'I don't judge, except to say what's on or off the subject.'

'Not ever?'

'Not the sort of judgment you mean.'

The prisoner sighed:

'And this is all it'll be?'

'Not quite. There'll be some tests too. Try to relax about it. I know it's difficult in here but just try to relax and concentrate while you're in this room with me. You were doing . . . fine.'

'Will we do the tests now . . . is this one?'

'No. Another day. One thing at a time. What were you saying when I interrupted?'

'I'm not sure. Can I stand up?'

'Of course. Why shouldn't you?'

'It's not "why shouldn't I". It's the business of asking. It's part of the rules . . . like the way the screws go potty if you don't call them "sir" and all that. Sir?'

'Yes?'

'Are you new?'

'No.' He coloured and was angry and felt it and saw no reason why he should be embarrassed. 'What were you saying?'

The prisoner walked to the spyhole. He peered through at the officer on the far side. Only the screw's eyes moved, a tightening, a focussing, but it was enough. Who do you think you are? What do you think you're doing? Sit back down and get on with it.

'Your spyhole hasn't got a flap.'

'Before.'

'School . . .' He smiled and took his seat. 'There was one boy who wanted to be friends . . . others later but the one at first. What an ugly child! He had glasses and nobody else much liked him and he said he was the R.C.M.P. Stupid!'

'Did you like him?'

'No. It was never a question of that.'

The listener made another note.

'What happened?'

'I don't know. He had some silly ideas. He used to trot around the schoolyard making sure it was okay and everything.'

'And he wanted you to join in?'

'Yes.'

'Did you disapprove?'

'Not really. I didn't think anything, one way or another. It was just the silly way he went about it . . . he used to run along sort of lopsided, slapping his harris and shouting, "Heyyyo!" and "Hupder"'; the prisoner leaned forward on the desk, looking steadily into the prison psychiatrist's face, 'and also . . . also, he only ever took one route.'

'You said there were other friends later.'

'Yes there were.'

'Tell me about them.'

'They were okay.' He looked quickly at the spyhole. 'I haven't finished with this one yet, though . . . you see, he had to stop doing it.'

He paused. The prison psychiatrist knew he was expected to ask 'why?', but he couldn't do so. In a natural conversation outside, yes, but not here. Here it would be a surrender of the initiative. He had surrendered enough initiatives to this man. More was not possible. Instead he turned his pad again, face down again, then face up again, as if for a sign in the sentences there. There was no sign, and he had not (he thought 'of course') expected any sign there.

'You see, the older kids used to play football; more of a sort of legally sanctioned bundle, it was, really.'

'A bundle?'

'A ruck . . . a fight. It was a very profound football, sort of stripped bare. One gang would gather at one end of the yard and the other at the other and then they would rush at each other, going at it for twenty minutes or so and stuck in like madmen.'

'You played in this?' Matter-of-fact.

'No . . . no. I was much too young then. I'd be stood by the wall near the bins or that, watching R.C.M.P. doing his circuit only this time, the one I'm talking about, he overdone it. Got out of his depth.'

'How?' Despite himself, and even though he knew he was allowing himself to be led, the listener's curiosity overcame what he thought of as his professionalism, and he simply followed. He was facing away from the barred window.

'Like this,' the subject smiled. He took his time, looking at his listener's bony long-of-finger hands stretched across the pad and the tips of the index fingers resting on each end of his pen. He looked to the man's eyes, blue and not at all the coolness that he would have expected. What would he have expected? He didn't know, but the blue long-look eyes and a slight crinkle at the sides for friendliness but firmness gave a feeling of humane-ness that, as soon as it touched him, he had known was missing in him now. Himself, in this place. Even the chaplain didn't, though he wasn't letting any sky-pilots get their claws into him. Not at this stage, the bastards. It's my path and I'll tread it, though, as I look at his carefully shaven face and beautiful hands I know (painfully) that I have put this behind me now and did some time ago. The prison psychiatrist saw the smile and mistook the silence that followed for something else. He found the smile suddenly pleasant and matched it inside himself.

'Two of the football players had a run-in, the usual sort of thing with kids. Suddenly there are kids all around and fists flying between the two. Ha! It's funny how you remember; I remember the girl next to me blew her nose on her school-skirt. Up comes R.C.M.P. "Heyup!" he says, and stops his horse. I remember one boy had his knee in the other's face, and then the one underneath bit it.' He leaned forward, placing his palms on the desk. 'The knee, you see. He bit the knee . . . so there's this guy hopping about holding his knee and screaming and the other one gets up all ready to put in the old coup of grace and drop him when Wealwaysgetourman jumps in.'

The psychiatrist-listener realized that an air of unreality had penetrated the story. It was an invention. He should not have allowed them to wander like this but it had been pleasant for the moment. He was used to it and knew that there was only one course open to him. He pressed the button on the desk.

'I think that's enough for today. You'll be here again on Thursday.'

'But look sir, the point is . . .'

The door opened and the prisoner stopped. The prison psychiatrist held up his hand, flat, towards the warder. It would be, he had decided, a kindness to allow the prisoner to continue with his story, his fiction. The psychiatrist was a good and friendly psychiatrist and he saw no reason not to give the prisoner this kindness. In a few seconds the iron grip of the institution would embrace the prisoner within itself, and the man would be subject to the pungency of slopping out and overcooked greens that the psychiatrist knew so well from his own visits to this place. The warder stood silent behind the prisoner.

He began again. 'R.C.M.P. says, "You mustn't" and the big animal says, "What?" and R.C.M.P. says, "Hit!" and the animal stuffs him one, pop! just like that, and he goes down flat on his 'arris, all big plopping drops of blood in his hands and his binns on the floor beside him and him blubbering on and on.'

'Have you finished now?'

'No . . . no, you see there's a point to this . . . I never did become friends with him, not really, not for that game and it was the only one he was ever interested in, even as he got older.'

The prisoner stood. He pushed his chair neatly back into its place before the desk.

'You see, sir, you see . . . yes, you see, I decided there and then never to become a policeman, not even a Royal Canadian one who'd been stuffed and mounted.' He knew the screw would give him hell for this when they got outside, but . . . but!

But the big dozy lump couldn't do a thing, wasn't allowed a bleedin' word in here. Trick-cyclist rules, okay. 'The point is,' and he grinned, 'policemen have to wear big hats, and I told you before, and I hated wearing me titfer.'

There was a silence, then the psychiatrist said, 'Thank you, that's all,' to both prisoner and warder.

The warder, who thought the comment was addressed only to him, ordered the prisoner to leave the room and wipe that smile off his face.

When the door was closed the psychiatrist walked over to the window and released the blind. The sun had gone in again. The psychiatrist saw the bars on his window, and far beyond, past the cell block, some bird of prey hovered high over the common. It was too far to see what type exactly, and, since the common was known but not seen, it was impossible to see what held the bird's interest.

The prison psychiatrist leaned his hands on the window ledge while he watched. Suddenly the bird swooped, dropping from sight behind the cell block. Soon it would be dark. He turned from the window. God! but that bastard took me. Maybe from the beginning. Maybe. Maybe it's all a waste of time. It felt like it. Cunning . . . pure bloody animal cunning. How could you write that in a court report?

'The subject comes on as thick as the door and would like (I think) to be considered slightly barmy. But the court should know that he is cunning, cunning as hell, and determined not to give anything away. My recommendation is that you hire some superior warders, or at least some with their fucking wits, excuse me yes, fucking wits, about them before you sling him in the chokee for a good long bit. I know I'm not supposed to talk about sentencing but I can think of no way of finding out for the moment whether there's any reasoning behind his heinous deed and cannot believe I am alone in this since the creaking-boot bobbies you've set on him can't find out either. For the moment we have to presume, sir (yes, Hicks; *sir* . . . I have to say it too), that there is some gross fault in his informal socialization at least and – time will tell, only time will tell me this – he exhibits a few of the symptoms of a psychopathically violent man. In short, I don't know if he's barmy or not, and he's not helping me to find out. I think we ought to treat him as if he is until we find . . . ' I can't say that! I just can't say that.

To rid himself of the idea of the imaginary court report the prison psychiatrist visualized his signature, 'Signed, Michael E. Cummings, Prison Psychiatrist' (I won't bother putting all my stupid useless letters after because they don't seem to have stood me in very good stead standing stood for the moment. Their magic, sir – again – doesn't seem to have worked on Hicks).

For some reason, having imagined up his signature, Michael Cummings couldn't imagine it away again. I'd better not imagine this place up or it'll never go away again, and I'm only forty (forty-one this year but not till December) which means that, statistically, I'd have to live with the image of grey drab stinking dump Wandsworth for thirty years . . . damn it all, there goes my social commitment for you. Why did you take it on then, eh? For more money and my new wife pregnant (not yet) to support . . . and the other cow too with her payments still left for the same bloody thirty years, I suppose. I haven't been very successful, I know. I should have took another speciality, hand-holding G.P. or bone-grinding (let us grind much red) . . . come on. Get it in perspective. You aren't here just for the money.

Michael Cummings gathered his papers and prepared to leave. It was too early but there wasn't much he could do here except write up his notes. He knew it was bad practice but he wasn't going to write up the notes now. His wife would be there at home and they had a family planned. He'd have a bath and drink a scotch and then write up the notes, which is better than here and then . . . well, they had a family planned.

He looked at the pad before he put it into the briefcase. 'Has nostalgic wish for old order.' Oh Michael! How can you be so stupid? This is all rubbish, and even if it weren't, what's a phrase like that meant to mean? What were you thinking of when you wrote that? I should have stayed in the hospital. The money's better here but these people don't need me. The courts don't need me. They need me to *say* something, regularize it. I'm expected to give an account of their . . . of their what? This man's condition isn't social, it's medical, this one's isn't medical, it's social. I ascribe you the status 'bonkers', do you ascribe me the status 'medicine man'? The courts give me that status. Will you? *Can* you? What's in it for you? A high security slammer as opposed to Broadmoor? You understand that . . .

good, let's start. Tell me about your childhood, Hicks. Bloodybloody Hicks.

Michael Cummings slammed the door of his office for temper. For being took. For the papers in the bag under his arm. He thought he'd better improve his temper. He hoped that his wife was in a good mood or at least not in a foul mood and he hoped that the family planning went ever so well tonight. Ever so well. This evening. I'm not waiting for tonight. He ignored the 'Good afternoon, sir' from the screw on the landing. Screw the lot of them for now.

Chapter Two

On Thursday, after lunch, Michael Cummings sat behind his desk and studied his written notes on the prisoner. It doesn't work. He refuses to take his own position on. He's intelligent, alert. He exhibits, perhaps, a certain goodfellowship in immediate relationship . . . exhibits, definitely, a profound disrespect for his immediate circumstances . . . perhaps, if there can be keys, this is the key. Perhaps. Perhaps the man would be serious today. It is possible to make too much of a lack of application, Michael Cummings knew. But he isn't the type of person (*type* of person?) to show all the signs of a detachment, a lack of involvement in his own destiny. That would explain the deed, the lack of involvement would explain the deed, okay; but where is the trigger for the lack of involvement? The family? Childhood? His failure at getting and keeping work? Perhaps, no 'perhaps', he *would* have recognized that society has rejected him. But is the taking of vengeance on one member anything other than a social response to social rejection? There seems to be no medical condition except . . . except. Except he is puzzling and I don't know yet and shouldn't try to judge yet or even think on it. I should just listen for now, oh I must be tired, I must. There is no pattern really. Too many parts that don't belong.

Though Michael Cummings was willing to accept that there are plenty of patterns with which psychiatry in general and Michael Cummings in particular were not familiar, he also believed (more intuitively, perhaps, than he felt he should) that behaviour must be the mirror to any man's mental state. It *has* to be, he thought, my whole science rests on this. What other indicators can there be? What other expression is open to us?

Michael Cummings had discussed such questions at great length as a younger man but now, in his maturity, the arguing was as nothing and the practical consequences of a man's deeds and his ability to possess 'mens rea' seemed to be all that he, Cummings, was required to answer. 'You have (have not) the ability to possess a guilty mind.'

Perhaps it is possible to make too much of a failure to take tests seriously. Other people take them far less seriously. But in him it *means* something. If it's a gesture and the other business was a gesture too then there's no question of what I must say but I have to get the background to the gesture, I have to know it was not an expression of a psychosis, that what ails you is not medical. It's important . . . if it is . . . if. You don't seem able to help.

Perhaps I'll give you the status you want. What is it by the way? Have you found a way of letting me know? I'm much too involved in you but any preference is possible, whatever we can present to a court on your behalf; me medicine man, you cuckoo. You outgame my games, me cuckold . . . no no. That's not fair. Maureen Elana would never allow her man to suffer such a fate. Not over some silly pf16 tests. We have a family planned. Sometimes this office is so untidy and I can't find a thing in it, Elana, and I'm sure the screws peep through the hole in my door that I haven't got a flap for and am told I'm not supposed to have one for. There, see, Hicks? If you'd give me some of that we could get right down to business. The rest could be a formality. You don't have complete command of your actions (but I will only say this if you agree not to let on no one else does and even that's not true. What sort of concept is no one else? No sort). I'm not in the mood for any clever dicky nonsense from you.

'C'min!'

'Sir.'

The warder was dismissed. The prisoner slouched in the chair before Michael Cummings.

'Same again, sir?'

Michael Cummings did not reply.

'Something wrong, sir?'

There was a long silence.

'Didn't I do it right, sir?'

'There's no right and not right in this matter. What I

eventually write about you can make a great difference to where and how you serve whatever sentence is passed. That's what you and I are about here. That's why you have to take it seriously.'

'I know that sir.' Hicks clasped and unclasped his hands, then looked intensely into Michael Cummings eyes. 'But they're going to give me a right turn, aren't they? All I can see is that the best thing for me is to sit back and do me bird. I'm not interested in mucking about here.'

'You have to be. You're here.'

The prisoner stood. His fists were clenched tight at his sides and his face was white now.

'Look mate, it's nothing to me, got it, nothing. I'm going to cop one this way or that. I'm up for the fucking cup. I don't want to do bird but I have to. I don't want to play your silly games and I *don't* have to. Got it?'

'Sit down.'

The prisoner sat.

'Finished?'

'Bollocks.'

'Don't swear at me. That's the second time.'

'What are you going to do, lock me up?'

'I'm not your custodian. I ask you to show some respect because I show you respect. You don't shock or hurt me with words like "bollocks".'

'Bollocks.'

'But you do make things deteriorate. You make it harder for me to work. If things aren't clear to me I can't make them clear to the court.'

'Doesn't matter.'

'It will do. If not now it will make a difference in time to come, when you're considered for parole, say, or for prisons which have different regimes. These people look back to each and every paper that's written on you. Even years later.'

'Sir?'

'Yes, Hicks.'

'Sir I know another geezer that's done the games.'

'What games?'

'The tests, then. Your ones with the cards and that.'

'We don't use ones with cards.'

'Well they did on him. A right case, he was. He's in for doing something nasty to kids. I'm not sure what, but the screws dropped the word and every time he took a shower he got a kicking.'

'Where's all this going, Hicks?'

'Well, the lady trick-cyclist shows him the cards and all that, the inkblot ones.'

'There aren't any inkblot ones used, I told you. And there are no women here. Concentrate on the business in hand.'

'Okay. But just let me finish. She turns up one card and he says . . .'

'I know. It's an old one, Hicks. Tell me about your family.'

'I don't want to. I already have.'

'Again then.'

Hicks shook his head violently.

'Tell me about your friends, then.'

'What friends? Who has friends in here?'

Start at a positive place.

'The school again then. You said who wasn't your friend . . . who was?'

'No one. Why don't you ring the bell, sir?'

'We'll just sit here a while. There's no rush.'

They sat awhile.

'I can see rats rushing round your desk.'

'Yes. They're there all right, Hicks.'

'And now they're turning blue.'

'Yes, they are.'

'I think one's going to bite you.'

'Yes he is, there. He's done it now.'

'You're worse than me.'

'The police say you didn't know him.'

'I did have one good mate, when I was a kid . . . a little coon he was. We were right good mates and then I went to grammar school and we lost touch completely.'

'You say he was a West Indian?'

'I said he was a little coon. He came from Homerton, born and bred.'

'And you came from Hackney too?'

Hicks pointed at the desk. 'It says there. You've read it.'

'Yes.'

'Anyway, we lost touch,' he giggled, 'until a funny thing happened. Only a couple of years ago. I'd been living out of there for quite a bit, nothing posh, just a bedsit. I was driving through the old area, just taking my time, looking, when I notice that old bill have got a jamjar full of our coloured brothers pulled up on the side of the road.' He laughed out loud. 'It was so funny. One minute these two flatfeet are standing there being very calm and talking into their radios. Now you've got to imagine, sir. The four chocolate drops are standing beside the car while one of the coppers is poking about inside it, planting drugs or whatever it is they do. Suddenly he calls his oppo over. No sooner does his mate start to walk towards the motor when, pop! the four chocolate drops take off like someone's put pepper on their tails. Cor dear, laugh? There's the two blue-bottles shouting into their radios, holding onto their hats and running about. Then one runs back to lock up his own motor, up comes a Ford Cortina with four huge mateys in it, as if anyone didn't know who they were,' he leaned forward, holding his palm up, to show he was giving Michael Cummings an intimacy, 'they might as well have "Filf" written on the back, but of course by now our coloured brothers had had it right away.' He leaned back in the chair and smiled. 'Right away. I drove round into the Kingsland Road and in the first phone box I see this short figure hunched over the blower and trying to keep his black boat-race turned away from the street.'

'Boat race?'

'Face ... he didn't want anyone to see his mush. So I laughed. I stopped me motor and went and knocked on the door of the box. "Oi!" and he's trying not to look round. I knocked again and shouted, "Oi! Car thief! Come out!" He was as pleased as hell to see who it was, old Claude. See, it was me mate from school, Claude. I said, "You'd better get in me motor, 'fore ol' bill sees you."'

'You'd done him a good turn?'

'What do you think?'

'And he's your friend since then?'

'Not really. He disappeared a while back.'

'He let you down, then?'

'No. He never let me down. He was a good mate. He would never have let me down.'

'Was?'

'Was. I won't see him no more.'

'He won't come here? He doesn't know you're in trouble?'

'That's right. He won't come here . . . I made a mistake earlier, sir.'

'Go on.'

'About the rat.'

'Yes?'

'It wasn't blue, it was yellow.'

'Have you finished?'

'No sir, I haven't finished.'

Michael Cummings pushed the button for the warder.

Hackney

Chapter Three

  pud
pud
pud
  pud
pud pud pud pud pudpudpudpudpudpudpudpudpudpud-
pudpudpudpud
  'Run!'
  Grunt.
  'Ru-u-unn!'
  'Yam!'
  'Faaaaster!'
  'Yam!'
dudududududududududududududududududududddddddd
dddddddddddddd
  'Aaaa-*ha*!'
Elf Hicks swept his arm across the front of his body, fist clenched and the arm close to his body; a vicious uppercut is delivered to some imaginary assailant. He had slowed to a trot now and he threw up his arms, palms open to the front. Elf ran on like this, as best as he could remember, like Seb Coe had in Moscow. He allowed his trotting footsteps to lead him off the tarmacadamed path. His knees buckled and he turned his shoulder slightly so that the fall onto the grass was softened some.
  Claude stopped beside him, first kneeling, then laying by Elf's side, heaving and sobbing for breath.
  'G'd'elp us,' Elf swore. He had enough breath now for some other sensation than breathlessness. There was even enough to swear with. There was heat in his cheeks and ears, both on and

in his skin, and now, as he recovered further, he became aware of slow trickles of sweat running past his brows and into the corners of his eyes. Elf blinked. He didn't have the energy to wipe his brow . . . so he let the sweat run; blinking being easier, blinking easy, blinkblink.

He closed his eyes and let his head roll to the side. Elf could smell the grass and he allowed the unseen green stuff to nestle against his hot cheek. He moved to rest on his side and could now hear the distant drone of a park tractor. It was puzzling. The tractor must have been there for some time but he'd only just heard it. He wriggled slightly for comfort, settling himself, and his own dampness returned to his skin. Elf shivered. The grass feel and smell sensation overtook him again and he opened his eyes.

'I . . . er . . . I.' Oh sod it.

Footsteps pounded on the earth behind him. Still Elf looked at the glistening brown brow of the man beside him. Claude opened his eyes and smiled.

'I what?'

'I've got two noses if I don't shut one eye.'

'What?'

'If I stare at my nose and I don't . . . oh! you know.'

Elf closed one eye and straightened the extraordinary Victorian monument that appeared to be balanced on the end of Claude's own nose. Claude stirred, sitting up, and followed Elf's eye to the obelisk.

'D'you know, Elf, everywhere I go there is some bleedin' great heap of bricks stickin' out of the ground.'

Elf did not attempt an answer. 'We live in a city', it's obvious.

The running pounding feet had passed behind them and now the sound was become faint. Elf rocked himself upright, feeling and enjoying the gut muscle hurts as he does it. He could see the girl now as she ran away, her footsteps far and her visual presence tantalizingly close. If Elf's head touches the ground does the sound increase? He rolled and tried his Red Indian trick. It doesn't work.

Claude was up again, trotting backwards and forwards and shaking his arms with his hands hanging loose. Elf stood.

'D'you reckon that then?'

Claude nodded.

'I reckon them all, mate.'

'Yeah, I know that, but do you reckon *that*?'
Claude turned and viewed the receding figure. He shrugged.
'Okay.'
'Okay? Just okay?'
'Well, nice then . . . you know I don't go for black women.'
'Your mother's one.'
'Not *that* like, the *other* like. You . . .'
Of course Elf knew and Claude couldn't be bothered to tell him. He let the sentence slip, walking away from Elf, and he began to jog at the side of the track. Elf caught him up.
'Claude!'
No answer, just a roll of the shoulder and a flash of green and grey and then tree and blue and Claude's fuzzbrown hair turns again and fills the space before and close to Elf's face, blocking out the grass and the grey ashphalt and losing the tree but not quite the coldcoldblueness of the sky as he came close. They stopped running.
'It's ah, right what I said . . . look.'
Claude took hold of Elf's shoulder and turned him to face the horizon over the City.
'Look. Those buildings, over there, and then over there, the Prince-silly-cods-Alby thing.' He had spun Elf away from the City to look at the memorial and now he spun him again to consider the skyline over the commercial centre, 'and over there, that great Natwest lump . . . they don't need them, y'know.'
'Oh yeah.'
'Yeah. They only put them up so that we know all the time, so we can't forget they own everything.'
'They do . . . what you gointa do about it?'
'Play better music than anyone can imagine . . . be the best U.K. born soun' aroun'.'
'And then you join them.'
'Not me no. No not me man. I wouldn't join 'em. I'd have reminders all around me,' and he swept at the sky with his hand.
'But . . .' said Elf and walked a few steps away.
'But?'
'Yes . . . but.'
Claude studied the building again, frowning for a few seconds before he spoke.

'D'you reckon that lot'd give me the two fousand four 'undred if I wrote an' asked them nicely?'

'I don't see why we can't let you have a paltry sum like two thousand four hundred, Mr Aint-got-two-brass-'apennies-to-rub-together. How long would you need the money for?'

'I'd say seventy years or so would see me through, how does that hit you?'

'Right in the profit and loss account, but don't despair, all is possible. You'll have to form yourself into a limited company and give us first option on your assets if you go boracic.'

'Fine. I don't mind bits of me getting sold off as long as they go to a good home. There's a titled lady in the Fulham Road who I reckon will give a good price for me handle.'

'Can't you be more exact, Mr Pissoff-there-aint-any-black-Russian-poets . . . the lady's name please?'

'Lots of them. We've got lots of fans down that part of the world and they'd all give it a good home, keep it warm an' that, entertain it on the fitted carpet.'

'As long as our debt is assured, sir.'

'No prob.'

'Then I don't see why not sir, just phone our branch and ask for Mr Bollox, he's our general 'itler in your area. Give my name, offer to brush his shoes or kiss his arse or something. You could say you were his long lost brother, Casper . . . he'd like that . . . no, I don't see why you can't have the money. It costs us a couple of grand to turn the lights on up there,' and he pointed at the building again. Claude winked and showed Elf the skin on his arm.

'Mr Bollox is a black bank manager . . . in England!'

'No no . . . tell him you're his half twin. I'm sure his mother got around. A wise child that knows his father.'

'Indeed, Mr Hicks. So you reckon I can have me money in the morning if I ask 'em to be aroun' in the dark tonight? Ha!' and Claude laughed and slapped his thigh. Elf looked more serious. It had been a very bad joke really, and he was more than doubtful of the wisdom of talking in such a way. Elf felt he should not now allow the joke to continue and he maybe should never have started it. Elf knew his friend could not expiate the problem just like that, by playing it up, acting the good but stupid piccaninny spanish-small we all expect our well-integrated blacks to be. It was insulting that Claude felt obliged to act in such a way with a real friend, but, since Elf had gone along this far, he could not complain.

'What are you going to do?'

'I don't know. I'd drive meself roun' the bend if I even started to worry about things like that. Don' worry, man!' and he punched Elf lightly. 'I've got other things . . . me music.' He brightened visibly at the thought of music. 'I've got a session tomorrow an' that's forty quid, but I don't have the other two fousand-odd and I can't see me doin' enough sessions in the next month to get to that.'

He frowned and Elf joined in with the seriousness, an emotion which he felt was appropriate.

'What'll you do?'

Claude shook his head and began trotting again.

'Claude!'

Trot.

'Claude!'

Claude ran on, speeding up suddenly. Elf stopped.

'Claude! Hold up . . . wait a minute!'

Claude is sometimes a little deaf.

The darkskinned girl who had passed earlier was running towards Elf now, passing Claude and slightly taller than him, with her feet flapping out awkwardly as she ran; as if she thought too much or was concentrating on the running too hard. Maybe her shoes are just a little too big for her. Her tracksuit and running-shoe outfit were new and, though she did not appear to be out of condition and was certainly (certainly!) not carrying any weight, she did seem to be unused to jogging, as if this was her first day's training.

Claude had his head down, shambling past her and growing smaller and smaller in Elf's sight as, equally, at each step he appeared more and more discontent. The girl loomed larger. Elfy rubbed his hands together and looked at the floor. It's no use going after the little bugger when he gets like that. He looked again at the girl. He ran his hands through his hair and pulled at his sweatshirt before he decided to call her.

'Hi!'

'Hi.'

She stopped and smiled. Although Elf's line to his mates would have been that this is what should happen if you give it some of that 'all right?', preen yourself, look cool (kool?), give her a drop of the business, the right line, he found now that the sudden confrontation with the face that was open and honest looking, wanting more, wasn't exactly what he'd been prepared for. Usually they smiled and ran past or came back with some sarcastic comment, and maybe he'd follow them and they would listen at the third or fourth attempt.

Elf suffered a momentary dislocation, a period during which his jaw and tongue seemed to be welded together.

'Yey.'

'What?'

'I say "hey", that was it.'

She smiled him a white tooth flash of a smile which was meant to say 'that's all right'. She replied, 'Hey!' and gave him a little wave, even though they were much too close for a wave to be necessary. It was courtly and a clear flirtation. Elf did not wave back.

'That's, uh, two circuits you've done, isn't it?'

'No.' Which contradiction took Elf as unawares as had her first response to him. He made to speak, but she nodded her head.

'Up there. I turned up there.'

Elf stepped closer.

'Where?'

'Up there . . . by the bushes. *My*, aren't your eyes bad . . . there, where Claude is.'

'Claude?'

'Yes. Your friend Claude. He's next to the bushes.'

Elf made to peer at Claude's back. He was trying to recover, but the girl spoke first.

'He's up towards the gate there now.'

Elf watched her carefully.

'Do you know my name?'

'No.'

Thank God for that.

'How do you know his?'

She made an open handed gesture in front of her body, typically African, and a knowing smile on her face . . . How does she know then? She hadn't answered.

'Well?'

She looked back to him, as if he'd disturbed some reverie, say, by accident.

28

'Well? Well what?'

'How do you know Claude?'

'Oh I've seen him around, at the Blues and that.'

She was not an immigrant and her accent was classless and placeless. She was ebony, pure shining carved ebony, and she smiled well and Elf was glad to have her attention.

'Oh I see. Well how do you do?'

'Very well thank you.'

'I'm Icks . . . Elfy Icks.'

'And I'm Nancy.'

'Fly me.'

'I'm not with you.'

'Joke.'

'Oh well, Elfy Icks . . . hullo.'

'Yes. We've just done all that . . . you, er, run up and down here a lot then?'

'Not really.'

'We do. We run most mornings, sort of hobby.'

'Yes. I saw you doing it.'

Elf watched her large brown eyes shine to and for him, just a second, and then the almond shape turns, foreshortened, and he's lost her attention and Claude is here, breathing hard and a big sweat on the end of his nose, like a dewdrop. He stops by them, crouching and resting back on his haunches, stretching his leg muscles and puffing in and out 'foom, foom' with a little rock backwards and forwards on the fulcrum of his ankles to accompany each 'foom'. He steadied himself then rose and looked straight at the girl. Elf spoke.

'You know Nancy.'

'No.' Claude wiped his brow.

'No Elf, not really. I never said I knew him . . . I've just seen you around at the Blues, Claude.'

Claude watched her carefully. 'I ain't seen you at the Blues.'

'Yes . . . the Phoenix Street one.'

Claude rubbed his brow again, this time less for sweat than for his thoughts. Past the girl, on the far side of the field, the obelisk, a memorial to Victoria herself rather than her beloved Alby, looked down benevolently on the Londoners. For some reason none of the ill-will with which he had earlier credited it was now apparent. He allowed his gaze to focus again on the girl. She stood before him with her lovely hands on her lovely hips and the soft blue woollen tracksuit touching her in all the right places. Claude was sure he didn't know her but she was *very* good looking. What the hell?

'Sure . . . yes, I remember you.' He made as if to study her again. 'You're not West Indian, though?'

'No. I'm English. My family are from Ghana.'

They paused naturally here, as if the word 'Ghana' had made some special mark. Elf looked at his feet and the grey asphalt below them, then the trees above, all dressed up in their yellowed autumn outfits, waving their finger branches at each other and touch touchtouching in the breeze. Elf caught Claude's eye for a second.

'I'm going to the Blues tonight, Nancy. Whyn't you come?'

'I will. I would have gone anyway. I have to see a girl. So!'

'Yes. So. See you there, then,' said Elf.

Claude frowned.

'They'll never let you in on your own.'

'D'you think . . . wouldn't I get in with Nancy?'

Claude began to walk away. He stopped and turned.

'But don' worry,' he winked, 'I'll take you.' And he turned again without waiting for any reply, as if the action had neatly tied up his morning. Elf turned to Nancy.

'Tonight?'

'Yes.' She smiled again. 'When?'

'Ten.'

'Kay . . . ten. See you.'

'Ten,' Elf repeated and hurried off to catch up with Claude.

The two men walked in silence for a few seconds, then Claude said:

'What's all this "I'm goin' to the Blues tonight" then?'

'I am.'

'Since when you go to de Blues. Tcha! You never bin before, Elfy boy.'

'If she's going, I am.'

Claude nodded thoughtfully. He did not speak for a few seconds, and when he did he stopped and looked full into Elf's face.

'What about your Carol?'

'What about her?'

'Nuffink . . .' Claude smiled, 'jus' astin.' He walked on. Elf followed, walking sideways and waving his arms as he spoke.

'You always get a J.A. accent when you're bullshitting, you know that?'

Shrug.

'Well you do and that's exactly what it is . . . bullshit. Carol didn't *buy* me when we got married y'know.'

'Six months only.' Claude raised his eyes to the sky.

'And if I didn't . . .' He stopped walking. 'If I want to go out I bloody-well will. All right?'

'An' where you goin' to be with your job if you take the evening off . . . eh? You'll end up like me . . . all sorts of bad news an' bad people wan' you.'

Elf shook his head.

'My problem mate. I'll pick you up. Half nine.'

They were nearing the street and they both stopped for a second, as if some unspoken agreement forced them to settle outstanding business before they left.

'It's not good, Elf man. Not good.'

But Elf had begun to run and he wouldn't stop, merely shouting, 'Half nine!' over his shoulder and then something else which was lost to Claude in a police siren.

Elf trotted towards the gate, one fist clenched high above his head, the ball safely in the back of the net, West Ham 1, Spurs 0. He raised the other arm to take the applause from the terraces.

Elf passed through the park gate. He stood still at the street-side, bathed now in the sound of the siren. The police car screeched around the little green patch in the middle of the junction, the faces inside young and drawn and wanting, it seemed to Elf, to be severe. As the sound faded the single, slow and sarcastic hand-clapping of the West Indian reminded Elf that his arms were still above his head – unsuitable once you're outside the park. No one would understand. In the park you could do anything, but in the street no one would understand a full-grown man's dream of scoring the winning goal in the F.A. Cup Final.

A lorry thundered past as if to reinforce the point – yer in the real world here, kid – a great, dirty, dust-covered tipper driven by a grey and dirty looking dust-covered man, a middle-aged man with his jaw firmly set and a blank expression in his face as he passed the roadside idiot with his arms held high. Elf turned, grinning, to Claude and dropped his arms to his sides.

Nancy, meanwhile, had stood on the spot for a few seconds

after the men had left. There was a problem; she'd have to run past the men to get to her car, and this would not be correct after all the finality of the last exchange. No . . . no, the car will have to wait on its own for a few seconds longer. She considered this for a moment and then turned to walk slowly and surely across the grass towards the obelisk. Nancy was pleased with herself and she allowed her training shoes to skid playfully on the grass.

Nancy sat at the foot of Vic's stick and watched Elf and Claude as they left the park. The avenue of tall plane trees stretched high, caressing the space above the men. A light breeze drifted across the open ground before her, ruffling the long, uncut, autumn grass; rust-coloured leaf spinning over brown leaf over yellow. A little dog jumps back surprised when the crisp bag he has been nosing suddenly becomes alive, catching the breeze and, cartwheelleaping, rolls happily away from him with the leaves. Nancy giggles. The little dog crouches low on his forepaws, suspicious and ready, he thinks, for whatever danger this new and unreliable stimulus may bring. His small boy companion retrieves the leash and drags the guardian off towards the gate and their breakfast. A small girl, perhaps his sister, tags along behind like some miniature Asian wife.

Beyond the boy and the dog, the breeze reached the trees; and they waved again, releasing a few bearers of the arborial gold. These drifted down to Elf and Claude, the walkers.

Even at this great distance Nancy could see that Claude was dragging his feet through the fallen leaves. Elf was crabbing along beside him, waving his arms and expounding on something; something vital. The little maybe-Asian-wife had changed direction and was walking towards her. Nancy became aware of the two-tone siren of a police car moving quickly along the Old Ford Road. The car raced along the perimeter of the park, and she could see the flashblue flashblue light; the side stripe, strawberry flavoured mivvi (jam sandwich, coppers call them), red fluorescence stipple-brushing the grey faces of the Hackney houses as it sped behind and, from Nancy's viewpoint, between the trees.

Elf and Claude reached the road. The noise of the street, their natural environment, Nancy thought, waited patiently for them. The lines of trees curved together at the gate, gathering themselves as the road turned and the trunks clumping close in a conspiracy to conceal the two men from her. The siren, live and buzzing street-side music, accepted them neutrally and naturally from the girl's gaze.

The perhaps-miniature-Asian-wife reached Nancy.

''e nicked me money,' and she sniffled unconvincingly.

'Who?'

''im . . . me bruvver.'

Nancy stood.

'Hey! Hey you!'

The boy with the dog stopped and pointed at himself; what, me?

'Yes! . . . You there! Do you have her money?'

'What?'

'You heard me young man . . . give it to her.'

The little girl ran towards him.

Nancy sat, satisfied. It had been a good morning. Now she was alone in the brief green grass and red leaf interlude from the city. 'Victoria Park belongs to me' . . . well, this bit does. She looked down at the knees of her tracksuit, absently picking at stray wisps of grass that had attached themselves to her. She stopped, then brushed herself clear with two determined and decisive strokes of the hand. She stood and walked towards the gate. She passed the boy and girl on her way. They were deep in negotiation and the puppy was running free. When she was some hundreds of yards past them she heard the boy call, his voice drifting with the breeze, faint and light.

'Hey! Hey! . . . Hey missus!'

She turned and waved. Both children were waving happily.

'Hi!' she waved back. 'What do you want?'

'Get stuffed!'

Up West

Chapter Four

'Your Carol', as Claude had referred to Elf's wife, stood in front of the display window of a large babywear shop in Oxford Street.

She was a pretty young woman with mid-brown hair and blue eyes. She was in her very early twenties and the prettiness had stayed with her even though her skin had lost its teenager shine since her marriage. She had also, during that same six months, gathered a little fat on her hips, imperceptible to those who saw her daily but it was there, Carol knew, and she could verify it on a weighing machine if she ever needed to. Carol never needed to.

She wore clean but ill-matched chain-store clothes, an acrylic (85%) and woollen (15%) jersey . . . C&A's, a wholly acrylic plain black skirt . . . Marks and Sparks, and an uncomfortable bright mauve coat that had been fashionable (she'd thought) when she had bought it a year before but was now something of a liability since it would 'go' with nothing else she owned.

Carol moved sideways a little to gain a better view of a pram; a large blue-paint and well-sprung-coachwork pram of the type not much used now, she knew, but she thought it would be *so* nice to have one when the time came for – 'when and if,' she corrected.

Carol caught sight of herself in the window, a tired-looking girl, she thought, as the image she controlled tipped its head sideways and stared steadily back at her own sideways-held head. She fingered the image's hair as she spoke to herself: 'Oh I do wish it were longer or shorter, it lays so badly and always looks greasy this length'; and she mused for a while on her image, ignoring the goods in the window and standing with her head tipped still.

A small, smartly dressed man asked her, in an accent that sounded as if he had an inverted tongue, if she was busy, miss, and would she like to go to . . . .

'No I'm not!' though she meant, Yes I am! . . . busy, that is. Carol's tone was sufficiently outraged to intimidate the little man, who, Carol noticed, was not shaven for all his crisply creased trousers and the fat gold chain around his wrist.

He stepped back, a stare, before he walked away moving slowly at first, as if nothing had happened, now shaking his head, as if 'How should I know why a young Englishwoman behaves strangely on the street? . . . I've done nothing . . . these Western girls have the reputation but are . . . what is the word? Without prediction.'

The spell had been broken as Carol had turned to answer, so that she must leave the shop window image to finger its own hair until she returned the next day. 'Maybe I won't go back again and it'll have to stand there with its silly short-and-long hair in its fingers forever . . .' and she smiled at the power she had given herself as she moved slowly and dreamily along the thoroughfare, her mauve coat unbuttoned, a large green plastic bag hanging loosely from her fingertips. Now the power over the image had left her and she felt as if it were *she*, Carol, trapped behind the glass in the babywear shop and the sound of the traffic and people were muffled by the window that contained her senses . . . yes! they are! And she touched her hair again with her fingers to prove that she could do it and stop and do it again if she wanted and when she wanted and that she didn't depend on a girl turning up to free her again tomorrow. Carol didn't want to depend on another shopgirl.

She had worked all morning as a shopgirl and she knew that she should step lightly and gaily on her afternoon off. She should be a not-shop-girl with all her might while she could. She should get out, get away, go to a park or a quiet and pretty street, have a coffee . . . go home. No! not go home. Don't go home Carol. I can't stay in that little room. Okay, go to Primrose Hill then, and look down on the world. The zoo! . . . no, I can't afford the zoo, even though I like it that much. I could go to Peter Jones' and sit in their coffee bar and spin on the stool with my coffee cup in my hand and fur coated women next to me and Chelsea my oyster for the moment until I finish and put my cup down.

I must buy some vegetables for supper . . . oh but no potatoes, or only a pound for Elf (and she felt herself to be fat of hip again and really determined herself, 'only a pound for Elf'). I could go to a museum . . . no, that's indoors.

Carol moved to the kerb, then skipped between the taxis clutching the green plastic Harrods bag close to her breast, so that her things didn't spill from it or jangle even. Why bother? It's all rubbish anyway . . . and she allowed the bag to drop and hang loosely in her hand again. She walked into Bond Street station and bought a ticket to Bethnal Green. Carol had known she would do this, even as she'd allowed herself to drift in the reverie.

As she descended into the bowels of the station she thought of the big pile of ironing and of course there are Elf's overalls to do and the unwashed breakfast things steeping in the greasy water, eugh!, cold now, and I bet he hasn't touched it. It's the adult thing to do, I should go home and I beseech you in the bowels of Bond Street, think that I may be mistaken.

Carol was doing what she thought of as the mature, or adult, thing, what responsible people do; but as she settled to wait for her train the feeling settled beside her that each time she did the 'adult thing' a little of her spirit was lost. As the grey train rattled and roared into the station the feeling encompassed her and held her in its arms, kissing her gently on the cheek, and she was sad. Carol rose and entered the carriage.

Technical considerations apart, the principal difference between the various parts of the London Transport Underground system lies not in the characteristics of the area through which it passes nor in the general passenger who will descend (usually) from the street to the train, but in the quality of each area's 'nutters'. These are the real users of the Underground: dull-looking, meat-and-two-veg of the human race, who don't simply *travel* on the Underground but, each time they will enter a carriage, tread the boards, so that each journey is a minor Shakespearean tragedy, and the distance between the stations is the backdrop to the pain and (sometimes) ecstasy of a true dramatic experience. There is, of course, plenty of scope for variety in a system as large as the L.T., but it cannot, surely, have been chance alone which has ensured that each carriage in each train is supplied with at least one fully paid-up 'nutter', and that each of these unfortunates is as different from any other as, given the basic rules of human morphology, is possible.

South Ken, for instance, will provide two women in full Moslem regalia, hundreds of feet of dull black cloth swathed about the large bodies while the shiny black yasmaks wiggle up and down as a sort of counterpoint to their chattering jaws. They settle in a corner, silent for just a second while they arrange themselves, murmuring quietly and not even seeming to pause one to listen to the other. The train halts and they find themselves a hundred feet below the marbled halls of Knightsbridge. They leap up screeching and begin to bang on the doors. The few seconds' extra separation from the shop consummation seems vital. Perhaps it is.

Seven Sisters, should you venture so far, gives us not Seven Brides for Seven Brothers but three small and decrepit looking men, near derelicts who shamble into the carriage. One falls asleep wedged under the armrests of a long, bench-type seat, his greasy rag of a coat gathered about himself for comfort rather than warmth. Maybe he thinks someone will steal it. The other two share a can of Carlsberg Special and begin to argue loudly over the *Sun* newspaper's banner headline, 'Black Mob on Rampage', maybe things'd be good if they weren't here, the government should send them home for good, there wouldn't be any unemployment if they weren't here, mugging and causing trouble. Things could be like they were. The casual listener watching the down-and-outs may muse on this and think, as the stinking creed of another time and another part of Europe seeps about the car, that this trick is an old one and has been played on the working-class too many times. They should know better, if they ever can learn. A look at their clothes might provoke the thought, '*When* are things ever any good for the likes of these?'; one of the men slaps the folded newspaper against his bony knee so that his body says, if his mouth will not, 'never . . . never yet'.

They will travel to Brixton and back on the Victorian Line, three or four times if they're lucky and no ticket inspectors board. In winter they will have stayed comfortable and warm and in any other season just comfortable, and they will rest for a while and have their chat.

Surrey Docks spills in two builders, suited-up in their Sunday best and full of the best, the two arm in arm and sharing intention on a coarse-looking poor woman who seems to be disengaged in some vital part of her nervous system, unable to turn without leering a smile of pain, first to one man, then the other. They travel like this, three on a double seat though the train is not crowded and Miss Cut-and-squeezed grapefruit turning her ugly face and squirting her ugly language to each, turn in turn, turn, turnabout. Her pain looks worse as she tries to walk, though it may not be pain at all.

As the train draws toward Whitechapel the men become angry suddenly, arguing across the front of the woman, the high-chortling (warbled, Sean) West Coast Eire voices pitched in temper, one to the other and ignoring her because their pride is the subject and much too important. 'It's you!' 'No! It's you, Osian, after all, wasn't it me that asked her this far?' and they stagger angrily to the doors, faces red and eyes shining, jabbering in their own front-of-tongue and lips-possessed English until the doors wheeze wide. The men continue on the platform, standing still and shouting. The woman sits silent, empty, aghast on the ribbed wood Whitechapel L.T. seat which has been inscribed for a long dead footplateman. She leans back on the dead man's brass plate while the men raise themselves to fever pitch in their unreasonableness. The pretty flower she had troubled to pin to herself for the occasion lies sideways now and the doors slam shut and the carriage they have left is quiet. The train begins to return to New Cross.

As Carol's doors slammed shut in Bond Street she was reminded of all these images she had seen and she was aware that this new journey might bring her some strange sight or perhaps intimate some sorrow which did or would sit beside each of her fellows and perhaps embrace them as her own sadness at her fugitive youth had embraced Carol.

She closed her eyes for composure and, as she opened them, was aware of her green bag of toot hung awkward, so that she stuffed it between her knees. She saw ⟶ιe signs, 'Unwanted hair?', 'Join the Transport Police' and 'Type in two days'. She dared her gaze to descend and saw two old women sitting shoulder to shoulder before her, one in a fur coat, one in a make-believe fur coat. Fur-fur had puffy eyes and a scarf carefully arranged so that she, Carol, could see the Hermès mark. Make-believe was fatter though without the puffs. She wore bright pink lipstick. Blue lines above her eyes darted about like little neon fish as she blinked and looked about herself. She did not appear to be wearing make-believe fur because she was an animal lover.

Both old women were grasping crisp and newly-filled carrier bags to themselves. They jiggled about in their seats without laughing and the train rocked its way to Holborn. They tut-tutted to each other (smiling, 'he's a bit touched, dear') when a young man came in and sat at the end of their carriage speaking rubbish very loudly to himself. They catch Carol's eye and stop smiling. The man shouts 'Me!' and they smile again. The young man begins again, secretively at first, now a politician's whine, pitch nasal high at the back of the throat.

'Durdledurdledurdle,' spoken low, 'I said!' shouted and now low again, 'Durdledurdledurdle.' He stopped suddenly and stared very hard at the floor before lifting his head and shouting 'Me!' with his finger jammed to his chest and now softly, 'Me.' He began to play with his greasy knotted hair, mumbling to himself. Carol smiled and the women gave her an ugly stare and the women and the young man left (thank God, Carol) at Liverpool Street.

The train filled with the indigenous 'nutters' of the East End, no commuter Havering-atte-Bowers free yet, it's too early, no office girls and no fat ladies loaded with shopping, just half a dozen people in cheap clothes and with tired bleary eyes. Shiftwork eyes. There was one interloper with a business suit sitting as if he had a bad smell under his nose, well he has, thought Carol, the rest of him's there. He kept staring at Carol's knees so that she took the bag to her lap again and kept her legs tight closed and closed her eyes also because it isn't far and she won't have to stand it for long. It's better not to look back if you can. It's only one stop.

Carol rose without looking at the business suit again. As she climbed to the street she was dusted by a dirt laden breeze that touched her face for just a second as she impeded its way to the tunnels. Then she was in the light and Carol saw that everyone about her looked just a little 'touched' (perhaps) and just a little trodden down (for sure). She caught sight of herself in a tobacconist's grimy window, no posh Oxford Street polish here. She saw she was like these people and, she could also see now, that none of them was 'nutty' but just poor and struggling and had their teeth gritted tight just to survive. Carol gritted her teeth too and trod the path to her tiny flat and used the determination to put the picture of the pile of ironing to one side again.

'Who's here?' she whispered.

'Who do you think?' and she walked to him,

'Hello, darling,' kissing his cheek. 'Aren't you supposed to be at work?'

'Blew it in.'

'Oh Elf!'

Elf turned on the sofa, holding his paperback above his head and presenting his back to his wife.

'Elf.'

He sighed and dropped the book to his chest.

'What?'

'What happened?'

He shrugged.

'Well, what's going to happen?'

'Nothing.'

'But you've only been there for three weeks.'

''s right.'

'But what if you lose your job?'

He shrugged again.

'I've got to go out tonight, anyhow. I've got business to see to.'

'What sort of business?'

He picked up the book and made to read again.

'Elf?'

'I'm going out with Claude.'

'You're not going to get into trouble?'

'No.'

'Is he still . . . is he going to get you involved in one of his "deals"?'

'Leave it out, girl. I told you, we've got business. Leave it.'

'Have you phoned your work?'

'Fuck my old boots . . . shut up!'

'Elf?'

Elf threw the book across the room, scoring a direct hit on the clock. He settled down with his palms behind his head, laying back on the sofa.

'Guderian was a Panzer general.'

'What?'

'Guderian was a Panzer general. Madrid is the capital of Spain. Things are easier to lift up if you use levers.'

'Oh Elf please.'

'Some things are easier to lift up if you use lovers,' he looked at her suddenly, 'very profound, that one, and I didn't even mean it to be. Cheese is heavier than wine. It's a long way to Brighton and there's a geezer at work who thinks it's downhill there and uphill back. It's further still to Scotland. No doubt that cunt has never been there because he can't stand the thought of pedalling four hundred miles uphill. I hate stupid jobs. I was expelled from school for popping the science teacher, there, right on the chin,' and he smiled suddenly, leaning forward and tapping her chin with the gentlest blow from his fist, allowing the knuckles to stay against her soft skin for just a second. Carol smiled in return.

'What *are* you talking about, Elf?'

He stood and walked to the window. The street below was empty and he played with the dust on the window-ledge for a second before answering.

'I am listing, Carol, the things I know. Reciting,' Elf jammed his forefinger against his temple, 'what's in here.'

She allowed him his few seconds of drama before replying.

'Do you know the phone number of your work?'

'Yes. That also.'

'Then go and phone them. Think of a reason.'

'Yes, ma'am.' He saluted.

'And you can't get out of it by clowning.'

'I'm not, ma'am.'

'Well, take things seriously.' She was quiet for a second. 'You'll lose this job too. You don't behave as if you love me, Elf. I bet the washing-up has been left all day.'

'Oh leave off!'

'Well it's true. Say I'm pregnant?'

'You're not.'

'But we don't know. Say I am?'

Elf ignored the question. Every time she's two days late we have to go through this silly performance. He began again.

'Bodegas are in Westerns and so are cantinas and lariats. Dustin Hoffman is in at least one Western and John Wayne is in lots of them. I've paid the tax on me jam jar, I don't have to worry about that. Sam Cooke got his for bunking someone up. The carpet is blue or it looks it. And you, Carol, my love, are not in the puddin' club.'

'Be serious.' There were tears in her eyes.

'You. I'm off.'

'No, Elf . . . where?'

'Just out Carol. Cool. I'm going out cool. Cool out.'

And, taking his jacket, he left.

'Will you phone your work?'

But the only answer was a door slam. Carol crossed the room and watched from the window as he made his way down the street. He moved with a grace which, she was sure, he would have denied having if she'd told him of it. She loved his ease of movement as she loved his awkwardness in the world, I do, I do, Carol thought. She turned and sat in his place on the sofa. The binding of the paperback Elf had thrown was split, so that the pages were spread around the floor. One large clump was still attached to the spine, glaring up at the plastic dome of the clock cover, swung open by the impact and dented but not broken. Carol said aloud:

'The book is broken but the clock is not.'

Now I'm playing his silly game. She closed her eyes and stretched her legs before kicking off the shoes and swinging her feet up onto the sofa. Carol lay back. Oh sod the washing up. Now I *am* playing his silly game. But sod the washing up.

Camden

Chapter Five

Derelict sites. Bomb sites. People call them bomb sites, though many of the people so calling were born long after the last bomb of the second war was dropped. Nowadays it should be 'council sites', not 'bomb sites', though they are derelict in any case, purchased for some grand plan during the sixties or seventies and left to rot while councillors do their sums again. Acre after acre is left as such throughout the city, nor pressing need nor party allegiance can overcome the inertia of the profit and loss account. Nettles gather at the mouths of broken water pipes, split-concrete platforms and eighty-year-buried pebble aggregate revealed now and moss grown; miles of corrugated fencing wends its way across a city of homeless and badly-housed families, unemployed bricklayers and carpenters, unused materials and . . . derelict sites.

A little road runs uselessly between such corrugated fencing walls, yellow street light cast and broken glass crunching under the tyres of a white Triumph rolling slowly along the cratered asphalt. A can is squeezed for a second by a tyre, then spins, clattering, to the kerb.

Small black boys are playing cricket across the street, peering for the rubber ball in the electric light and a lamp-post chalked for their wicket. They stop to allow the car to pass. Three tall and dark-fronted houses interrupt the fencing, a door thrown wide suddenly illuminating the junk that fills what should be their front gardens and the crazy-cracked plaster upon what should be an imposing portico. A shadow of a man steps onto the street.

'Here. Not that one, the first.'
'It's empty.'

'Probably going on in the back. I'll go and check.'

Claude left the car and crossed to the first house. Elf drove to the end of the road, deliberately letting the Triumph's tyres squeal as he turned. When he reached the house again Claude was standing with a young white man. The man wore a greasy army jacket and had shoulder length hair. Elf wound down his window.

'What's happening?'

Claude shrugged.

'You talk to him.'

'What's the score, pal?'

'Huh?'

'S.P. . . . what's happening?'

'The streets are on fire, man. The world's running down and people are starving but you still come round here burning up fossils.'

Claude walked towards the car.

'See what I mean? Cuckoo,' as he passed. Elf moved closer to the man.

'Where's the spades from next door gone?'

'Oh . . . the spades. Cool they were. Cool spades.'

'Yeah yeah. Where've they all gone?'

'Good music and score herb anytime. Fucking cool.' His eyes narrowed suddenly and he held a skinny arm and hand, palm up, towards Elf. 'Cool spades. They weren't burning no fucking world up man. No. No streets burning with them. All good Moroccan stuff.'

'You wouldn't know it if they hit you round the head with it. Where've they gone?'

'Good squat ours and them next door, then the pigs came round and blew them, know what I mean?'

Elf knew what he meant. He nodded, I know. I know you've seen Easy Rider once too often. And your pupils are too wide. Comes of sitting around with the lights out.

'Where've they gone?'

'How do I know? Back to the pig bin.'

'No. The spades.'

'Come on, 's a waste of time. He don't know what day it is.' Claude stood with the car door open. 'Fuckin' hippy, straight out of the time machine. 'e finks it's 1968.' He put his forefinger to his temple and screwed it back and forth.

'Where've they gone?' Elf asked, with exaggerated patience.
'Away man . . . you're pigs as well, ain't you?'
'No.'
'Yes you are. Aren't they Mary?' He spun quickly to face his house and shouted the last sentence. A woman stepped from the shadows. She wore an Indian cotton dress, though the September night was chill, and her face was thin and pale. Elf was surprised, unreasonably, that there was no child clung to her breast. Cop that, he thought, these old dugs; earth mother lentil soup and curried wholemeal nourished drooping breasts. Bloody Harry Krishna. Harry harry, harry harry, Harry Cripps' goal from the halfway line. Who was that against? Too long ago.

'These are pigs. I asked them and they admitted it.'
'Come in, Jamie. Come in.'
Jamie sat on the little wall in front of his house. The woman was old enough but he could only have been a kid in 1968. He shook his head.

'Pigs. Set the streets on fire. Pigs. Never leave you alone. Sheer pollution.' He shook his mainline head again and wept a little.

'Sheer murder,' muttered Claude from the open car door, loud enough to be sure of being heard. Elf joined him and they drove off, stopping by the cricket players.

'Oi!' Elf called. They ignored him. Claude leaned across.
'Hey spa! Where am de blues now?'
The batsman stood upright, signalling the bowler to stop. He walked over to the car.

'What?'
'Where de blues go?'
'Babylon shut dem down. Dem over de railway now,' he pointed with the bat, 'same road, 'im call Verdun Street, but de same road, 'alfway down. Number seventeen.'

Born in London, Elfy boy, born in London and never seen the sky over the West Indies. Hark at him.

Claude leaned across, holding out his hand, which the boy slapped, palm on palm.

'T'anks.'
'Snuffin,' and he sauntered back to his crease, rubbing the prized-possession willow face of his bat with his free hand and waiting for the car to move on.

The house in Verdun Street had lights on and looked a better prospect. Elf dropped Claude and drove around the corner to park. He didn't want his car seen outside. When he reached the house again there were two big men in the hallway, the door half open and Claude negotiating with them. The conversation stopped as Elf entered and all three men moved into a room off the hallway. Elf followed, then down some steps and he was in a surprisingly large room. It was quite crowded and the sweet smell of cannabis filled the air. The lights were very low. There was reggae music and a short youth in a leather beanie tinkering with the record player as if it were a full sized sound system. He muttered to himself, half in time with the music, as if he were toasting with the best. In his head he was. He looked up and smiled at Claude.

'Hi man.'

'Hi.' And Claude waved back and this was repeated many times as people recognized him.

At the far end of the room a trestle table was stacked with drinks; Red Stripe, dark and light rum, gin and coke. Orange juice. A man stood guard over the drinks, an older man than most in the room, say, fifty; smooth-shaven, balding, good clothes and a big smile. He had one hand on the stack of Red Stripe and directed his smile to Elf, who was sure he didn't know the man, but, since the smile so obliged him, approached the table and asked for two beers.

'Two poun'.'

'That's a bity tasty, isn't it?'

'Every drink is one poun'. No one asked you to come.' Still smiling, perhaps broader, even.

Elf paid and took the beers. Claude stood with a group of men in a corner and Elf approached.

'Ta,' accepting the beer, 'this is me mate, Elfy Icks. 's all right, know what I mean? These gentlemen, Elf, are . . .' he paused, 'acquaintances through business. Gentlemen?' Smiles all round. They ought to call this a 'smiles party', Elf thought, no blues in sight. Not a one.

'Number One here is . . . number one.' The man to whom he referred leered forward, a tall man with a serious half-caste face, pock-marked from a disease that doesn't exist any more. He wore a green and yellow rugby shirt and rasta hair. He looked about the same size as any three rastas Elf had ever seen put together. He also looked aggressive, most un-rasta, that, and Elf decided that it was only a hair-style for Number One.

'An' Little Maurice,' who was even bigger than Number One though much less sombre. Between the two enforcers was a small, pinch-faced man in a cashmere polo and new blue jeans. He wore dark glasses (in here!) and a cigarette protruded from the corner of his mouth.

'Sir John Bright.'

The small man held out his hand and gave Elf's hand a cool, firm, unsweated, grip.

'Sir *Lord* John Bright,' he corrected, 'but, as you are a friend of my friend Claude, you may call me "Sir", Mr Icks.'

'Cheers.' You're a right cheers mate. Cheers mate. And Elf shook the hand again. He had a smile like a nurse shark, and Elf realized that the man was a West Indian of Asian extraction, very dark of skin but definitely, as West Indians call them, a Coolie-boy. It was very strange to find a Coolie-boy in such an obvious position of power amongst his West Indian fellows.

He spoke. 'Claude here tells me that you are in search of a certain girl of African origin.' Sir Lord John Bright smiled again and Number One began to nod for some reason, his improbable black cap wobbling on his thatch of hair.

'Uh, not in search. I said I would meet her,' he looked into the man's eyes, 'if that wasn't taking too much for granted.'

'No no. Any friend of my friend Claude here, as I said. Anyway, in search . . . you will find her, I believe, in the back room.' He grinned and Elf half-expected to see more than just one row of teeth upper and one lower. 'Cherchez la femme.'

Nancy was, as promised, in the back room. She and a paler skinned girl were sitting at each end of an old, large, wooden table. The room had at some time been a kitchen. Both women had glasses of drink before them and there was a cat and crumbs on the table top. The paler girl had her elbows amongst the crumbs and was leaning her head moodily and lazily on the heel of her hand. Elf thought, she may be a whore, though he had no good cause to think so.

'Elf!'

Nancy stood.

'Himself.'

She held out her hand, a peculiar gesture, he felt, but he took it and shook it.

'Hullo.'

The lighter skinned girl was given a mumbled introduction and left.

'How are you?'

'From this morning?'

She laughed. 'Yes, it is a bit cliché-ed but we have to start somewhere.'

She wore jeans and a white blouse, no jewellery, and looked, if anything, better than she had in the morning.

'Yes. We do. Well, how are *you*?'

'I'm fine, Elfy Icks. Is your friend here?'

He nodded. 'Outside, talking with some heavy looking J.A. characters. D'you want another drink?'

Nancy didn't get a chance to answer. At that moment the door crashed open and a large white man, all mild ginger hair and staring eyes, staggered into the room. He was talking as he was walking and he turned, suddenly, shouting, 'Y'raas!' into the empty doorway before kicking the door shut. He staggered across to the sink, turned the tap on and ran the water over his face, shouting through the stream.

'Mi Jamaica born. Jamaica!' He stood again and wiped his face on the front of his tee-shirt, revealing a pale and ginger-hair-matted paunch as he did so.

'Mi J.A. born. Pure J.A., not return-home Englishman. Trenchtown, ya hear?'

Elf nodded that he heard.

'Trenchtown! An' dese men mekin',' he stopped, breathing heavily, and took two uneven and unbalanced steps to their table then slammed his fist down between Elf and Nancy. The cat sat up, startled, then leapt for the floor.

'Untruth! Untruth!'

Elf rose. 'Let's get some more drinks, eh?'

Nancy rose also. The man slammed his fist down again on the table-top, but before Elf could reach the door it was opened by Little Maurice. He did not speak but walked calmly and firmly across the little room and punched the ginger-haired man in the stomach. It seemed, to Elf, strange, as if it were the only thing to do, a slow film, Peckinpah violence, remorseless and seemingly inevitable. Ginger swung back wildly, the film speeding to normal now, and then Number One was in it too, taking one of Ginger's arms and pushing his head at the table top. The cat had made it under the sink and Elf felt he wasn't a bad judge. The two big black men were laying into Ginger and him shouting 'Trenchtown' and then coughing the next part. His head hit the table-top hard. The make-believe-sound-system toaster pushed past Elf, beanie bobbing, and leapt onto the man's back, too late now, since he'd subsided – succumbed, more like, to the persuasion of Little Maurice and Number One. The three helped the ginger man gently to the door, then threw him into the night.

Little Maurice turned, grinning, and Number One bent to pick up his fallen black hat from the floor. The cat hissed at Number One from his place under the sink, 'Maybe they're going to eat me now.' He stayed very firmly in his corner, claws bared.

'I'm sorry. I wonder if you'd take a drink with me to replace those overturned during this unfortunate incident.'

Elf turned. Sir Lord John Bright stood in the doorway, all ease and double-glazing salesmanship. He grinned, nurse-shark again, first at his boys, then at Elf and Nancy, before turning to wave at the bar.

'Drink on me. Please.'

The middle-aged barman was stood beside Sir Lord John Bright, the last line of defence before the great man himself should have to dirty his hands, and he went scuttling back to his bar at a nod from his master. Elf and Nancy returned to the main room. Claude grinned but did not come over.

'What is your job, Elfy Icks?'

'Factory. And you?'

'All sorts of things. I'm a sort of freelance. What about Claude?'

'He's a session man, or at least he is while he's still got his electric joanna and all the gear.'

'Has he lost it?'

'He will do if he's not careful. He borrowed the folding stuff for it off some nasty characters and now he can't get it together to pay them back.'

'People here?'

'I don't know. It wouldn't surprise me. Whoever they are they've got the hump.'

She was quiet for a second, then, 'Couldn't he have got it on ordinary H.P.?'

55

'No.' Very firm head shaking. 'Who'd give people like me and him things on the drip?'

She smiled and squeezed his arm. 'I would.'

'Well you'd be wrong to.'

'Can we get some of that?'

She pointed at one of the men in Claude's group, spliffing. The mini-toast was standing there too, surveying the contents of a wallet which was clearly not his own. He looked up and scowled at Elf.

'Go and ask.'

She did, coming back with the joint held tenderly, cupped in her hands and offering it to Elf.

'I don't.'

'It's dear.'

'Yes. It's not that. I just don't.'

'Okay. Just as well, fifty pence a puff.'

'Always is, one little one like that.'

'Could I buy a bigger lot here?'

'I thought you came here regularly.'

She drew at the joint and fixed him in her gaze. 'No. Just a few times. I don't really know people here. Just acquainted.'

'Sir Lord John Bright?'

'It's his show. Nobody gets by without getting to know him . . . say I wanted to score a bigger lot of herb, who would I ask?'

'Me.'

'But you don't smoke it Elf.'

'I can get it for you.' He nodded to Claude. 'But don't you ask him. I will. How much?'

There was no reply. Suddenly there was a lot of banging in the hall. Some shouts. The door was thrown wide to reveal the large ginger-haired white man again, something of an expert in dramatic entrances. His face had paled and there was a large cut running vertically on his forehead, half-dried and ugly-looking. There were dark stains on the front of his already filthy blue tee-shirt. He held his arms up, consciously striking an apocalyptic pose.

'T'ieves! T'ieves!'

Elf supressed a laugh at the melodrama, then looked around for the mini-toaster with the wallet. Surprisingly enough he was nowhere to be seen. Surprise. It looked as if Little Maurice and

Number One were going to give a repeat performance when a little boy ran in, pushing through the crowd.

'Babylon!' He stood panting for a second, then took a good lungful. 'Dem here!' His eyes were popping and this time Elf did laugh. He realised he was alone. All over the room packets were being dropped to the floor. The crowd was silent and serious. The ginger white man was pushing his way about the room, shouting still and grabbing people for a moment, taking a look, sometimes a question about his missing wallet, then releasing roughly. No one attempted to stop him. The music was stopped. Claude came over.

''s best you go. Leave by that window and there'll be a side entrance. I clocked it on the way in.'

'What about everyone else?'

'What can they do? No point in panicking. Take her with you.'

'You sound like "Shane" . . . okay.'

Claude was in fact wrong. People were struggling to get through to the ex-kitchen, and, presumably, the rear door. Sir Lord John Bright had disappeared, though his enforcers had not and were, like Claude, calm and unruffled. The whore-looking paler-skinned woman who had been with Nancy was pushing her way to the back of the room with her stilettoes above her head. Babylon, which Elf had long since realized meant the police, were making no attempt to enter. The ginger man screamed on and on about his wallet.

Elf climbed through the sash window, dropping from the ledge onto a sunken path, then turning to help Nancy down.

'*Such* a gentleman.'

'Ssssh!'

The path was strewn with rubbish, broken glass, wood, odd pieces of metal, a dismembered bicycle frame and some very definitely bio-degradable piece that Elf stepped in as he walked towards the tall wooden gate. He could see the reflections of the blue lights on the walls of nearby buildings, no sirens, and he could hear soft speaking voices outside the gate. He eased the bolt and slowly opened the gate. Some steps led to the street with a tall hedge, dark and menacing on each side. Elf's eyes were not yet accustomed to night vision. He turned and whispered to Nancy, 'We'd better just run.'

She shook her head but he moved quickly up the steps and

holding her hand. It was then, as Elf thought of it later, that the piano dropped on his head. He did not know it but he had met, for the first time, a certain Constable David Higgins of the Metropolitan Police, 'O' Division.

Chapter Six

P.C. Higgins was not the most successful ever member of the Metropolitan Police. He was a country boy, young, dark haired, well-built, and he had recently transferred from a county force.

P.C. Higgins had expected, and received, his quota of 'swede' jokes from the Mets, now his colleagues. What he hadn't expected was to be considered useless, or at best, inadequate. He was even more surprised to find himself acting out the part. Yokel. Yokel Higgins. He didn't mean to act it out but, as he found himself considered Peter Street Police Station's 'yokel', he appropriated to himself attributes of the 'yokel' which he could not, in fairness, be naturally considered to possess. This was at first unconscious, but then became moved from the unwitting to the unwilling, as if he were a man that stared into an abyss. Yokel. Swede.

He was unsuccessful, and his new colleagues recognized this. If, for instance, he was in on a 'pull' while riding area car (incident vehicle, in the Met, but Higgins could never cure himself of saying 'area car') his colleagues would always find a way of keeping Higgins in the background. 'Don't say too much, you wind 'em up.' He had to admit to himself (though never publicly) that he did 'wind 'em up'. A central London copper, with only a vague idea of the location of Highbury Barn or (worse) the Acklam Hall, was a 'wind up' indeed and started off any conversation at least half a sentence behind his suspect. Since the whole technique of even the most informal street-side police interrogation is always to posit the questions in such a way as the subject could only reply in certain pre-determined ways (each of which led to another, equally pre-

59

determined, set of well-tried suspicions and well-tried questions and answers) Higgins' half-sentence lapse made him appear simply . . . thick.

'Yokel' Higgins had experience, all right, but it was in policing an area in which he'd lived and been involved. Here he was not involved and frequently out of his depth. He couldn't be like the commuter coppers who descended from their dormitory suburbs each day to engage in a swift, sophisticated and seemingly well-rehearsed repartee with the natives. And so he felt inadequate.

P.C. Higgins recognized that the business on the slum steps was different, more awkward, more absurd even, than this.

The only occasion in the past on which P.C. David Higgins had been forced to hit someone seriously was when a local nutter had knocked on the glass screen of his old county nick. P.C. Higgins had opened the hatch and watched in horror as the man plunged a broken bottle into his own bared chest, pale stretched skin broken, curled hair and spilt blood escaping around the jagged edges; glazed of eye, unsteady on his feet, (though clearly not drunk) and screaming for the lights to be put out. It was mid-day. Anaesthesia was required, and P.C. Higgins, being alone in the little police station, had administered an appropriate 'clout round the ear'ole' (temple, more accurately) and then first aid as best he could: 'Wake up, you bugger, no, on second thoughts, don't.'

P.C. David Higgins was, you will understand, a sensitive man, and he did not sleep easily for some time after hitting a madman. This was because he felt it was wrong, and he exercised his mind over the rightness and wrongness of such an action for many sleepless nights.

London violence did not allow any room for the finer points of moral philosophy. There was no order to it, not even the self-inflicted self-hate of a madman order. If you took a 'body', say, some suspected person on the street, and it looked wrong, people would go for you. Even ordinary passers-by, nothing to do with it, *what's it to them*, passers-by would fight, sometimes verbally, sometimes physically. If you sounded too lippy pulling a carful of yobs the conversation would start with 'oo yoo slaggin' off, John?' and quickly descend into violence if you didn't keep a firm grip. You would be as likely as not to need the assistance of half-a-dozen coppers to sort out the resulting mêlée. This would mean a series of wry comments from the sergeant to come and at least one awkward interview with the Chief Inpsector, 'Sit down, Higgins' (in a creaky chair), to follow.

So it was that P.C. David Higgins found himself in an ''urry up wagon', a Ford Transit with P.V.C. screens over the windows and the whole of the southern half of 'O' division as his patch shared with six other constables, two 'whoopsys', an inspector (nominally in charge) and a sergeant (actually in charge). And so it was that they took a '9' call for Verdun Street – 'neighbour complains man berserk in house, origins Information Room 22.17, M.P. out' – and P.C. Higgins found himself on the broken paving stone, dog-shit and rubbish street-side waiting for some order from the sergeant or inspector and a small crowd of nearby neighbours (no one lived next door and no one wished to) gathered and paying attention to the blue uniformed officials who must know what they're doing. They *must*.

The sergeant had sought a rôle for Higgins in which he would not, at least, have to open his mouth.

'Stand there and don't let anyone out. Whatever you do don't go upsetting any of the bloody nignogs unless Mr Jenson or I say to . . . . Just stop anyone coming out and remember we're here for a white bloke. Play it cool and don't open your mouth unless you have to, got it?'

'Skip.'

'Good.' And the sergeant turned from his close and confident attitude to Higgins and re-erected the professional grimness upon his countenance which would reassure the ratepayers gathered to watch.

Two dog vans had turned out and another G.P. Transit and P.C. David Higgins had stood apprehensively in the shadows of his hedge while the lights flashed and the policemen murmured and the crowd watched and the 'guvnor' took his little posse to the door. Plenty of third-world shouting going on, y'raas, Babylon, raas claat! inside the seedy house and Higgins determined to keep his end up this time and not 'fuck-up, yokel, fuck-up. Another bleedin' swede-head fuck-up', his truncheon tucked up his sleeve so that just a handful of wood protruded past the cuff on the inside of the forearm. Higgins' fist grasped the four inches of protruding wood. He felt the sweat from his hand tacky against the polished surface and wondered if he should have the stick's leather strap wrapped around his wrist as he had been taught. The gate slid open and a white man (there can't be two, surely, in there) rushed him.

Almost by reflex P.C. Higgins brought up his arm and stick held within and the next thing he knew a black girl was standing on the steps looking at him sullenly while he tried to pick up the prone figure of his victim, an untidy heap on the steps. The body was very heavy and very unconscious, oh I didn't mean to hit him that hard. Oh damn.

The sergeant came over, his attention attracted by the groaning behind the hedge and the sight of P.C. Higgins' serge bum poking free of the bushes in a most unofficial attitude as he bent to deal with the unconscious Elf. The sergeant and constable picked Elf between them and dragged him over to their vehicle, propping him against the rear door and holding on in case he fell over again. Elf's mind was in a half-light, seeing the street as a dazzling maze of yellow-burn sodium and wavy figures, some nearer, some further. Why is one of those sodiums blue? Why does it keep going on and off? I've never seen a blue sodium before. Some people with furred edges walked past, just out of reach and, for some reason, just out of focus. Two sharp-focus friendly men were holding him up. Wasn't that nice of them? Yes. He nodded and found it hurt to do so. Yes it is, isn't it *nice* of them?

'Bloody hell.' Sergeant Cobb shook his head as he spoke. 'Bloody hell. What did you hit him that hard for?'

'He rushed me, skip.'

'Well you stopped him, all right. Bloody hell you stopped him. Was he going to hit you?'

'I thought so.'

'Bloody hell. He won't be doing any more rushing for tonight. You'd better nick him. Put him in the van.'

'What for, skip?'

'What do you mean, "what for?" . . . so he can't run away, swede-head, why else would you put him in the van?'

'No, I mean nick him.'

The sergeant looked exasperated:

'Because you've hit him!' He dropped his voice again, realizing he must be discreet in front of the crowd. 'Because we can't have people going around with lumps on their heads without being able to account for them,' he released the semi-conscious Elf and took Higgins' lapel, 'it's . . .' Elf groaned and slid down the doorway of the Transit, lopsided because Higgins kept his grip; Sergeant Cobb pulled him upright, 'bloody messy, swedehead. People will want to know where he got his bump'.

'No skip, I meant, what under?'

'Under . . .' the sergeant paused, swearing softly to himself. A fracas was taking place inside the house and he should not be getting tied up here, 'Section 5 or something. I d'know. We'll sort it out back at the factory. Who's the bird?'

'With him.'

'Bring her as well . . . miss?'

'Yes.'

'Get into the van please.'

Nancy did. She was quiet and calm and had been all through the incident. She mounted the step into the van and was promptly pushed out again by a whoopsy to be searched. Nancy submitted. As she looked over the W.P.C.'s shoulder she could see a minor riot going on in the doorway of the 'blues'. Three policemen were struggling up the steps with Number One, then two more with a now quiescent 'Trenchtown Ginger'.

A Rover was parked with its headlamps on the crowd, an eerie thin circle of gawpers and more corrugated metal lit for a backdrop, regular and repeated shadow slip shadow past, after the untidiness of the crowd. One man came forward and claimed to have seen Elf attack. He was small and fat with a thin moustache and a rumpled looking face, well-slept in, a shiftworker roused for the entertainment. He was much shorter than the young Sergeant Cobb and looked up into the official's face with the expression of a dog with a fowl in its mouth.

'What did you see?'

'That bloke. He tried to hit your boy. I seen it. I seen it *all*.'

'You'd better take his name and address. Handcuff your prisoner and put him in . . . and Higgins.'

'Skip?'

'Caution him. Do it properly.'

The chant began, informal by name though such a caution seems anything but informal: 'You're not obliged to say anything unless you wish to do so . . .'

63

Elf was mildly surprised, in his newly surfaced consciousness, to find that the constable was addressing him.

'Oh.'

He was pushed into the van.

Elf didn't really begin to recover properly until he was in the charge room, a room which had never seen a plasterer in all its ninety-odd years but was instead painted grey lower and pink upper thick gloss. Generations of thick gloss. There was quite a queue outside, most of the members of which were recognizable from the blues, and consisting of far too many people for the two detention cells and two interview rooms the station boasted.

It was Elf's turn. He stood with P.C. Higgins in front of the tall charge desk. The Station Sergeant, a grey haired and severe looking man in his late middle-age listened while P.C. Higgins went through his version of events. It sounded like a total fiction and Elf learned during this of his assault on a constable in the execution of his duty and being about to renew a breach of the peace. A baby-faced constable stood by the Station Sergeant's side. He seemed unwilling to catch Elf's eye. The older man glared at Elf all through the constable's tale.

When Higgins had finished the Station Sergeant asked Elf did he have anything to say for himself. No, he shook his head, no. I can't compete with him. He should have a job in Hollywood. Couldn't he speak up? No. Was he struck dumb, lad?

'No.'

'No what?'

'No I don't have anything to say.'

Constable Higgins read him a formal caution from a card sellotaped to the desk-top.

Elf shook his head again. No he did not wish to say anything *still*, and he appreciated (too well) he was not obliged to do so and that anything he said *would* be put into writing and *may* be given in evidence. Since he saw no stenographer Elf did not believe that what he said *would*, as the man said, *be put into writing*, or, going by their behaviour up till now, anything remotely resembling a true record of what he said would be kept. Elf decided to keep his mouth shut. The little he knew of the psychology of these people led him to believe that they needed some basis for their little fictions (he could agree with Higgins, for instance, that he had indeed been in Verdun Road and that he had walked between two hedges) and Elf was unwilling to provide it.

'I'll accept the charge, constable . . .' The sergeant turned to Elf. 'Name?'

'Icks.'

'Spell it.'

'H.I.C.K.S. Icks.'

'First name?'

'Elfred.'

'Spell it.'

'A.L.F.R.E.D. Elfred.'

'Ever been in trouble before?'

I'm not in trouble now mate, I've done sod all. Yes I am. I've still done sod all but a realistic appreciation, Elfy boy, would lead you to agree that you're in the soddin' merde, dans la chocolat right up to the lug'oles. Elf said, 'No.'

'Never?'

'No.'

He was asked for his age and height, asked to sign the book 'like it was the 'ilton'. Elf was shown a sheet of pink paper that listed his crimes, asked to sign it too and promised a copy when he left. He was searched and his belongings noted, coins of the realm to the value of fifty-five pence, seven banknotes to the value of seven pounds, one yellow metal watch, two key rings, one with two keys and one with three. The property was placed in a bag and taken from the room by the baby-face. He was asked to sign that the notes were a true record of his property and did so before being divested of his belt and shoelaces (he wore no tie) and led to his new home for the night. Elf looked up at the charge-room clock, eleven fifteen p.m. Some night out. Some pulling. Some African crumpet. Where the fuck had she got to when they'd left the maria? Where was Claude? Some luck.

Elf was 'banged up' in the little room, also grey gloss to waist high, pink gloss paint to the ceiling and that part white gloss. They must have the bleedin' stuff delivered by the tanker-full. There was a ship-type bulwark-lamp glowing on the wall. Some decorators! Glass brick window, dead of light from the night. Some night. Some luck. He lay on the bunk. Some luck.

Elf closed his eyes and fingered the bump on his head. At

least it's above the hairline. But ouch! it hurts. He opened his eyes again and looked around the room. He sat up. There was little furniture, a toilet bowl (with a screwed down seat and a chromed push on the wall for the flush, directly opposite the spyhole and unscreened), the bunk, a pillow and two grey blankets. Elf picked up a blanket from the foot of the bed. It smelled of old sweat. He stood and faced the door.

'Hoi!'

No sound to answer.

'Hoi! I said hoi! It's not exactly the 'ilton, is it?'

There was no reply, though he had not expected one. He tapped the heavy metal door with his knuckles. It was like tapping on the walls of the White Tower. A button on the wall was marked 'attention'. Elf stood stiffly to attention, then sat upon the bunk, smiling.

Soon he stood and paced the distance from the wall to the door, full-sized paces and then turning, pigeon-toe pacing the return. Thirteen or five, whichever. Elf sat on the wooden rim of the toilet bowl and stared at the door, which was wholly pink and stared a cyclops glare back. I wonder when I'll get out of this; that Carol'll give me a right ear-bending when she finds out, oo! (he clapped his hands together) fuckin' 'ell, won't she! I should ask for me one phone call, that's what they do on the telly. Rattle me tin mug against the bars . . . I haven't got a tin mug and there ain't no bars. I could have me call, though, clue the cuddles in, no. No. Get a brief. That's it, get a brief. 'Give me Perry Mason, operator . . . long distance . . . shadd*up* cop, I got money, I can pay. Oh, Hullo, Per? Yeah, 's Elf here, not bad mate, slight prob though. Down your alley, really.'

He stood and moved his hands forward to clear the wrists from the cuffs, Cagney style, and twisting his lips so that the imagined conversation slipped silently from the corner of his mouth. 'Yeah, the cops have got me banged up in Peter Street, yeah, Per, it's a bum rap. Yeah I know it's a long way, but can you come and spring me?' His beltless trousers slipped a little and Perry lost his chance to reply, just as Elf lost his pose in pulling at his trousers. He sat on the bunk again, stood immediately to adjust the waistband yet once more, then began to do press-ups and sit-ups until he collapsed, exhausted, face down on the floor. Elf crawled into the bunk, sweating coldly. The bump on his head was throbbing.

After some time the lock clicked and the door swung open, smoothly and quietly. Baby Face followed Elf along the corridor to the charge-room, then handed him over to two large and villainous looking men in civilian clothes. Elf walked between them to an interview room.

'Sit down, plase, Mr Hicks.'

Elf did. The room was large and airy, a long barred window near the roof giving, like his cell, onto the darkness. Four striplights, one flickering. Official table, biro scarred, 'Piss off, old bill'. The older of the two policemen sat opposite Elf, turning the chair to rest his arms on the back (he's seen Cagney too). He wore a suit and tie, fat stripes on the tie and the suit lapels slightly too wide, and the man stretched his arms forward onto the table, palms down with plenty of gold cufflink showing. The policeman had a smile-lined and friendly face and steady, sure, brown eyes. The younger plain-clothes man stood below the barred window, doing a 'moody' act, facing away from Elf and with his shoulders hunched slightly within a brown leather casual jacket.

The older man asked, 'Would you like a cigarette?'

Elf shook his head.

'Tea? Anything else?'

'Me belt and shoelaces. I dunno how I was s'posed to come to any harm with me shoelaces.'

The older policeman stood and tapped on the door, then asked Baby Face for the articles. He sat again, smiling apologetically.

'We have to take them while you're in the cell, Mr Hicks. We have to account for your well-being.'

'Pity your oppo, Higgins, didn't think of that earlier.'

The man smiled again and held up his hands, palms up and open. When Elf was belted of trouser and laced of shoe the older man opened a notebook.

'Let's see . . . you were arrested, or detained rather, leaving premises on which we suspected offences were taking place.'

'If you call a brick on the head "detained".'

'Ah now, Mr Hicks. That's a very serious allegation . . . I won't make a note of it for now, but we'll see how you feel as the interview progresses . . . . Where were we?' He leaned back, checking himself with his hands on the chair back before him and leaving the notebook spread on the table-top.

67

'And then you were brought here to be, er, *quest*ioned.'

Elf nodded, I was brought here and I'm being questioned, it's hard to disagree. 'I *am* being questioned. I haven't done nothing.'

The younger detective turned, a black beard, angry eyes and pulling at a woollen polo neck under the beard. He advanced and leaned at Elf from the end of the table.

'*You* cock, were in a place where drug dealing was going on. *Drug dealing*. Then, to make good your escape, you *assaulted* a constable.'

Elf touched the bump on his head but said nothing.

'For all we know you may have been one of the drug dealers. Perhaps a search would help.' He turned to the older policeman with a gleam in his eye. 'I'm sure an analysis of his clothes would show traces of cannabis. Come on you, take your clothes off.'

'What?'

'You heard me, take your clothes off!'

'Piss off.'

The bearded policeman pulled Elf upright by his collar, then began to drag him across the room.

'Take them off.'

'Ah . . . that's enough now. I'm sure it's not necessary with Mr Hicks.' The older policeman nodded at Elf. 'Let him go now, let him go. Sit down again, Mr Hicks.'

Elf sat. The bearded copper leaned over him again.

'*You* cock, are scum. *Scum*.' He walked away from Elf, a melodramatic swagger in his gait.

The older policeman, the *friendlier* policeman, flapped his hand dismissively at his colleague:

'People's emotions can, I'm sure you will understand, Mr Hicks, become exaggerated in a situation like this. Even your own, perhaps . . . anyway, enough of this. The fact *is*, Mr Hicks, we have very good evidence for a variety of serious offences against you.' He leaned forward. 'Imprisonable offences, you will understand. If we followed the path my colleague suggests, perhaps we would have evidence to consider for other imprisonable offences.'

The man said 'imprisonable' as if it were a word whose very sound was of great import, and he looked steadily at Elf each time he said it. The bearded detective leaned against the corner of the room again, pulling at his polo neck sweater still. He turned and said quietly, 'Scum.'

Elf ignored it.

'How do you feel about the police, Mr Hicks?'

Elf shrugged, how do you think?

'I mean, have you ever been in trouble before?'

No I bleedin' haven't, and what's more I'm not in trouble now. What's the matter with you lot? Elf looked at the older policeman; what's the point?

'No I haven't, Mr Whatever-your-name-is, and I think that once I get a brief I won't be in trouble now.'

Beard bounced across from his corner like a tag-wrestler, slamming his clenched fist on the table.

'You attacked a policeman!'

'I *didn't*!'

There was a long silence. The older man spoke.

'Do you take sugar in tea, Mr Hicks?'

'No.'

The man tossed a fifty pence coin at Beard's fist, which was still held in the position of table beating.

'Three teas, Brian. Two without.' He leaned back, pulling at his belly, and looked up at Elf smiling.' Three, better make it three without.'

Brian the Beard left.

'Cigarette now?'

'No thanks. I don't.'

'Well. That's good, anyway . . . let me see. This is a very difficult situation I find myself in. You see, Mr Hicks, I am not an unreasonable man. *We* in the police service, despite the press we get, are reasonable people. I for one, and I believe P.C. . . .' he consulted the notebook, leaning forward and allowing his head to nod as he read, 'Higgins, yes, that's right, P.C. Higgins, would not be happy to prosecute a man of otherwise blameless character for the one offence . . . do you see my problem, Mr Hicks?'

'Yes.' Elf didn't.

'Do you remember *exactly* what happened this evening?'

'I'm not sure. I don't want to say anything. The constable said I didn't have to unless I wanted to,' now Elf leaned forward, 'twice. Exactly twice.' He nodded his head each time he said 'twice', an answering nod to the copper's earlier. What a funny game. I'm as potty as this lot. No I'm not, but it was definitely 'twice' (and he nodded again), my memory's that good.

Brian returned with the tea-coloured liquid and was despatched, scowling and tea-less, to fetch Higgins.

'P.C. Higgins. How did you find Mr Hicks?'

'He was prostrate on the side steps of number seventeen Verdun Street, sir.'

'Yes. And then you brought him here to assist in sorting the whole matter out.'

'*Asked* him to come, sir.'

'Yes. Quite. And now he has assisted us, hasn't he, constable?'

'Yes sir.'

Bearded Brian left, unsignalled this time and still without tasting his tea, and the older detective pushed it to Higgins. There was a silence while the three sipped the teas. Elf suddenly realized what was happening, God that bonk on the bonce *has* slowed me down. He would not, he decided, deny them their way out.

'And that appears to sum it up as Constable Higgins sees it, Mr Hicks. Don't you agree?'

'Yes, er, yes I do.'

'Good. That's how you see it?'

'Yes.'

'Yes. Good. And since you've assisted us most fully perhaps you'd like to go home now, yes, Mr Hicks?'

'Yes I would.'

'Then perhaps you'll go with the officer and sign for your property.'

The detective stood and tapped on the interview-room door. The flickering neon failed finally.

'We'll have to fix that, Constable Higgins.'

'Sir?'

'The light, constable, the light. Report it.'

'Sir.'

Baby Face opened the door, being followed back down the corridor by Higgins as the detective held the door wide. As Elf followed the man stopped him, grasping the elbow and his face coming close to the prisoner-now-ex-prisoner's (nearly).

'One last thing, Mr Hicks.' The corridor was empty and Elf

was alone with the detective. 'You appear to be in a position in which you are singularly well placed to help us. Singularly well placed, with your contacts.'

Elf did not reply.

'My name is Detective Inspector O'Keefe. *O'Keefe*, remember it. If you want to talk to me, say if you come across something you think I might want to know, or something I should know, call here and ask for me. You don't need to give your name.'

'Yes.'

'Will you?'

'If.' I'll say anything to get out.'

'Yes. Just *if*. Just call and leave a message if you can. If I'm not here. You haven't got anything for me now?'

'No. I don't think so.'

'You owe me one, Alfred, you owe me one. Remember that and remember my name.'

'I will. It's Elf though. My name's Elf.'

'Okay. Elf. You remember me, Elf and I'll remember you. Mr O'Keefe, remember? And call if you think there's anything I should know.'

'Okay.' said Elf. He immediately set himself to forgetting the name; O'Keefe, relief, belief, bereft . . . *bereft*, there's one. Going going gone. Finished, no more to be seen or heard from. You can get your claws out of my brain for a start, Mr Relief-belief-befallen-upon-bereftness. Gone.

As Elf entered the panelled dark-wood foyer of the police station he saw Nancy. The outer door was swinging, resettling itself from recent use, but she was thoroughly settled on a bench underneath the notice-board, being personally surmounted by a drawing of a monkey assembled from the spare parts of a variety of higher primates and set-off, in true Scotland Yard style, with thick eyebrows and a heavy beard. 'Have you seen this man?' Elf smiled for the unintentional joke of the stupid notice and then more for the woman as she looked up.

'Okay?'

'Yes. Are you?'

'I think so. I didn't expect you to wait.'

'How's your head?' She stood close to look.

''s okay. There's nothing to see. What did he hit me with?'

'I don't know. Shall we go?'

71

'Yes.'

They walked out to the street.

Three floors above a bewildered P.C. David Higgins was trying to work out what had happened.

'But I was right to nick him, skip, you said.'

'You didn't nick him. You discovered him injured and asked him in to help with enquiries.'

'Yes. But say he comes back and starts cribbing.'

'He won't.'

Suddenly Sergeant Cobb stood. He walked around from behind his desk and stood very close to Higgins while he spoke.

'Look. Mr O'Keefe wants a snout among the nignogs. He wants to investigate very serious matters, *much* more serious than what we were dealing with here. Hicks may be what he wants. He won't do us any good if he's doing three months porrige for trying to belt you. So, David, with your assistance, he's out where he's needed.'

'And what about the charge sheet an' all, and the witness?'

'I'll see to the charge sheet. You talk to the witness. Buy him a cup of tea. Reassure him . . . *talk* to him, David. It's one of the skills you're going to need in this job.'

'I know, skip. I'm not new.'

'No. But you're new here. Take advice, listen, then develop the skills.'

P.C. Higgins was listening. He wanted to say that he didn't think it was right, or perhaps he wanted to say that he was sure that it wasn't. He wasn't sure. He felt conned, let down. He knew that if he did voice his doubts he would be safe from immediate sanction but his star, already waning in the Metropolitan Police, would sink still further, and if he failed to co-operate now he would have 'gone west' for all intents and purposes as far as his colleagues were concerned, just as surely as if he'd failed to take Cobb's advice on the slum steps. That. He'd done what he was told and now he was dropped even further in it. But maybe if he hadn't taken Cobb's advice he would have 'gone west' legally too, a summons in his hand and up in front of the Assistant Chief . . . oh damn, I'll never get used to it here. Up in front of the Commander. They don't have Chief Constables and therefore have no assistant ones . . . I'd have been sent up in front of someone though, if I'd got it wrong, on a blooming fizzer, 'Yes sir, no sir, where'll I pick up my cards sir?' P.C. Higgins had found the duplicity of the detectives in his old country force a shock but these were literally fantastic. The sheer deviousness of what he'd been inveigled into was appalling, and he considered this for a second before he realized that Sergeant Cobb was waiting for a reply.

'I'll go and see him tomorrow, skip.'

'You do that, David. You do it. I thought you'd gone asleep for a minute there.'

'No. Just thinking.'

'Perhaps you'd better sit down. Go downstairs and have a cup of tea.'

'Sarge.'

David Higgins was through the double doors and making his way downstairs. He was worried about Hicks. He thought he *should* be worried about Hicks. Higgins paused behind the firestop double doors on the first floor. The canteen's on the top floor, he thought, but that Cobb definitely said 'go down'. *I know.* Higgins had his 'Promotion Handbooks, Police Procedure' in his tunic side-pocket, brought along as a talisman, in case the skipper had started quoting at him and getting too tricky. Higgins lifted the paperback from his pocket, thumbing through for 'Powers of Arrest' and 'Prisoners'. *Ah* . . . 'Prisoners' . . .mm. He leaned forward to rest his arm on the door while he pondered, no rest being achieved because he simply kept going until he hit the floor, banging his elbow sharply and getting a smack in the face from the 'Promotion Handbook'. Higgins shook his head and turned sideways to look at a large pair of well polished shoes. It was the bearded detective. Higgins couldn't recall the name.

'See your body, Hicks, has been let out, then.'

The detective released the door-handle and held his hand out to the prone constable, grunting as he helped heave Higgins upright.

'By God you weigh some. Must be all that agriculturalizing you were doing before . . . that is you, isn't it?'

'Yes mate.' He bent to retrieve the book, feeling unreasonably angry that the book was scuffed and marked at 'Prisoners'.

'Still, you did well to run the bastard in. Feather in your cap that, y'know.'

'Thanks.'

'I reckoned we could've turned him right over. Bound to have had something on him . . . still. We'll get him again, eh? Make it stick next time. Just between you and me, it's only the D.I. getting a bee in his bonnet about having another snout . . . *gawd* knows why he's picked on this one . . . some bloody crap about keeping his eye on the coons instead of going in hard and reg'lar.'

'Oh.'

Brian the Beard was in full flight now, and he didn't care how many 'ohs' he received for reply. Oh.

'That's the only way to keep them down. Go in and wallop the scum, hard and reg'lar, so they know they can't bring their filthy drug-taking habits here. Go and pollute some other poor sod's patch.'

'Mm.'

'And the only way to convince them so they stay convinced is to . . .'

'Go in hard and regular.'

The beard parted to smile at Higgins.

''s right. You were listening. I thought you weren't for a minute.'

'Oh, I've been preoccupied.'

'Well don't be. Good nick and a good body. It's only because of people here wanting to pansy about fine-tuning their fucking image. Too much of that . . . still,' he slapped Higgins' upper arm in a friendly way, 'we'll make it stick next time. I've got something put by in the property cupboard for bastards like him, no ticket on it, know what I mean?' And, amazingly, the man touched his nose with his forefinger. Just like in a film, thought Higgins. 'The only trouble is, he's not on collators or C.R.O. That could have worked out embarrassing for him, the D.I. I mean.'

'And what'll he get for it?'

Brian the Beard looked shocked, even if it was only mock shocked.

'Only information. Don't be naive, son, clowns like Hicks haven't got any dough. But if you're lucky they'll either give you a lot on people that could use a favour or two . . .'

He paused for a second while another detective pushed past them in the doorway, nodding greetings to him. He leaned forward, so he could speak closely into Higgins' face. 'Or . . . a little bit on very naughty boys. Takes a lot of pressure off a D.I. if he's turning over the big bad lads on his patch every now and then. Trouble is . . .' and he leaned back for effect, much to Higgins' relief, for he had found out that his new friend had halitosis, ' . . . O'Keefe's got it wrong. Wogs don't respond to finesse. If he gets clever with them he'll just confuse them . . . know what I mean?'

Again the touch of the finger to the nose. Higgins nodded that he knew what was meant. He wasn't sure, but he thought he probably wouldn't like it if any more London detective's secrets were revealed to him. The man frowned.

'Here . . . what were you doing on the floor?'

'I was on my way for a cup of tea and . . .'

'Canteen's on the top floor mate.'

'I'm new.'

The frown lifted a little. That's true, he is new. Still, bloody funny. Better not say no more. You never know.

'Right then, Higgins. I can't hang about here all night. Good nick, that's all I was saying, really. Don't let yourself get worried about all the shit. Watch yourself, if you're new here. Buy me a pint if you've got a problem or want advice, all that.'

'Right. Thanks.'

The detective pointed.

'Top floor, canteen.'

David Higgins began to climb the stairs. As he climbed he began to worry again.

I shouldn't have thumped him but I wasn't sure what he was going to do and I thought he was going to thump me. Having thumped him I shouldn't have nicked him (it was *immoral*, and this word stayed with him, uncomfortably, for a few seconds) and having nicked him I shouldn't have let him go. I shouldn't have let myself be bullied, not in the first place nor here. I hope I don't see him again.

In the street, the subject of all the thumping, nicking, releasing and moral uncertainty in P.C. Higgins' mind took Nancy's arm and hailed a cab.

'We'll share?'

'Yes, your place or mine first?'

'One lump or two. Where do you live, Nancy?'

'Clapham . . . oh! What about . . .'

'What?'

'It doesn't matter.'
'Okay. Clapham, driver.'
'Big place. Whereabouts?'
Nancy told him.

Embankment

Chapter Seven

Elf stopped the cab at Blackfriars Bridge, I've got to get some air, I just must, I really have got to get out, we can easy get another cab. Any time. Nancy did not complain. They paid off the cabby and walked down the slope from the bridge, turning round and round at the City griffin and Nancy laughing at Elf's clowning, now I'm in it, now I'm not. City, Westminster, City, Westminster. Elf ran then, on the Westminster side of the griffin and shield, for a hundred yards or so. He left Nancy behind and was laughing for being free and for being free to run, and then he turned to wave at her, still laughing.

'Oh God I'm better here, Nancy.'

They leaned on the great wall, laughing still.

'I thought I was up for the cup in that nick, cor dear, I've never been so bloody nervous in my life.'

'Well you're here, now.'

'Yes. I'm here.' Elf stared at the river, a great heaving bulk of water, rythmic flow, on and on and twinkling under the lights of the south bank.

'Why d'you think Big Ben is there?' He pointed behind the south bank complex.

'It just is.'

'But it's not on that side, it's on *this* side.'

'Yes.' She smiled for him and Elf turned to the smile and asked, 'What's in it for you?'

'What do you mean?'

'Well, I mean . . . we don't exactly know each other. Why didn't you buzz off while I was in the slammer? Why did you stay?'

'I don't know. It's not very nice to ask me to say.'

'Sorry. I just think it's good of you. Do you know what happened to Claude?'

'I'm not exactly sure. A policeman told me they'd taken some of them to another station.'

'Did they catch him with anything?'

'I don't know.'

'But you waited for me.'

'Yes.'

Elf put his arm around her shoulders and kissed her cheek quickly.

'Why?'

'Oh *do* stop asking me questions. If it makes you feel any better because you said you could score some herb for me. I didn't exactly go to the police station as a volunteer, remember?'

'No.'

'Well I didn't, and they were letting us go at the same time, so don't go falling in love with yourself.'

He held up his hands.

'Don't shoot, I'm coming out . . . why d'you need me, anyway, if you know all those guys back at the blues?'

'They don't trust me. I'm African, they're West Indian. Anyway, I'm only on speaking terms with Sir Lord John Bright.'

'Are you joking, about the West Indians, I mean?'

She shook her head.

'No. Even your friend, I can tell. They're always suspicious of us.'

'Us English.'

'Yes,' she laughed, 'we English.'

They had walked now as far as Cleopatra's needle and the woman held his arm. Elf felt that the evening might yet prove to have been worthwhile. It might be yet, rather. He climbed onto the wall and stood with his back to the river.

'Aren't you going to tell me to get down?'

'Why should I?' Nancy replied, 'I'm not responsible for you.'

Elf hopped from foot to foot, now swinging his arms like a monkey, no you're not my keeper, but you can come and sweep out my zoo cage, now make-believe wobbling as if he would fall into the river.

'But if,' she went on, 'by some chance you should fall and dash your brains out below, I won't waste my time on you.'

'I'd drown, not bash me 'ead in, anyway,' Elf bent forward, hands on his hips, as he spoke, 'you waited at the nick.'

'I *didn't* wait, they kept me . . . anyway, that wasn't your fault. This would be.' She had put her hands on her hips as she spoke, mimicking him. '*That*, Elf, is the difference.'

He stood upright, laughing and cried aloud, 'Vive la différence!' before beginning a promenade along the top of the wall, a soft-shoe-Chevalier, 'Evrry leetle breeze sims to whesper "Louise"', then stopping suddenly and changing it into Elvis, swivelling his hips and screeching some dimly-lit memory fragment from *Girls, Girls, Girls*, (or was it *Summer Holiday*? No, don't be silly, that's the other one, whatsisnáme) and the African English girl stood wearing the coat he had thrown to her, the sleeves too long and enveloping her hands, which were warm, and she felt it, but still shivering a little for the chill of a clear autumn night on the Thames-side. Nancy giggled unselfconsciously at Elf's embankment act and a newspaper van drove past, throwing a gust of air which Elf rocked with, exaggeratedly, as if he was again about to fall in.

'And then a piano dropped on my head!' he laughed.

'Get down you bloody idiot!' a policeman called from the far side of the street. 'Down!'

Elf climbed down, then thumbed his nose at the back of the policeman as the man continued on his beat towards Temple underground.

Nancy called, 'Here, sit down,' slapping the wood of the bench on which she'd sat. Elf ignored it. His mood had been changed utterly by the intervention of the voice of authority. He leaned on the wall and gazed across the river, then stepped back, keeping his hands on the stone wall and dropping his head to watch his shadow on the pavement and then he could pick out the edges of the paving stones, butted, edge-edge to edge and edge, and Elf thought of the nineteenth-century mason or paviour or whatever they were called then, probably a change-trade navigator or navvy out of a job once they finished the Grand Union. Then Elf's eyes were more accustomed to the light below him and he saw the cigarette butts lain upon the paving butts, butt to butt to butt to butt to pink-stained lipstick-touched butt, brilliant pink, visible even in this light

81

cigarette butt which was not flattened as is usual but crumpled, as if whoever-she-was had taken the trouble to bend and use the paving edge (butt) as an ashtray for her cigarette butt, and bending so that her butt, or arse, U.K. style (rub a dub session version's 'raas') almost touched the pavement as she butted her cigarette butt, whenever that had been, maybe days and maybe weeks earlier. Elf looked at the ghost or residue of the woman's presence and action set upon the ghost or residue of the ancient paviour's presence and action.

 A breeze caused the street dust to sweep around the crumpled pink-lip butt and then on and over it as the breeze intensified for a second, but still a light breeze and gentle. Elf lifted his head to meet the air lifting and it touched his brow and brown hair. As he stood upright for the breeze Elf watched the river, thousands of shards of shattered light cast, scattered from the broken pot of ruined and pre-historic trees that we burn to gain this peculiar brightness and the brightness may belong to the metropolis but it's never, Elf thought, Metropolitan (O'Keefe, d'you hear? O'Fuck, I thought you'd gone away). It would be wrong for anyone to try to annex light —— Nancy sat patiently on the bench and watched Elf's back and thought that she did not know him well enough to comfort him and anyway didn't want to. If he didn't want to get into trouble he shouldn't go to 'blues' parties and hang around with people onto drugs.

 . . . though, once it's formed, 'electric' we channel it, or rather, someone channels it and it is subject to law, being brought now from the petrified forest far below and changed from a potential. If the bastards find a way they'll meter the air we breathe and stick clocks on our cocks, 'wipe that smile off your face, you're not due till tomorrer . . . name, address, size of piece'. Very plausible.

 The breeze dropped from gentleness to complete stillness, and though he did not bother to look down and check he realized that the pink-lip ghost was of a very recent origin since there had been no dust evident on it (though there would be now) and there had been other breezes breezing around here this evening so (Watson) the neat-minded woman had been here very recently ——

 'Elf.'

 He ignored it ——

a half hour, an hour perhaps. Maybe she was arm in arm with

some lover and the two fresh from an evening at the theatre opposite, or the N.F.T., a faint dew of sweet sweat on the woman's upper lip being chilled to the tune of a breeze that ceases as she bends. Perhaps the couple had come here to collect their car, no, *his* car, or at least this is usual, and if she'd gone to the trouble of putting on lipstick maybe she'd get fucked when they climbed out of their BMW in their suburb or maybe she would before if she isn't his wife, mind the gearstick while you're on the long strokes but it won't matter when you're on the short strokes as long as she doesn't get her 'arris caught up in a revolving ash-tray (butt trapped with pink-tipped butts) and you could even end up getting your foot stuck in the glovebox when you come to the tragic bit and lose *all* sense of proportion, socking it to the maps and even scuff shoe scraped across the front of your 'Mastercover' policy pamphlet that you've been keeping neatly in there in case something ever goes wrong with your bright and shiny-new jamjar. If it had 'Mastercover' it would be BL, of course, not a beemer, and then he would have had a Rover and driven her fast and English away to their dark place or bedroom or both.

'Elf.'

She could always be a wife who bothered to put lipstick on because she had a husband who could be bothered to take her to see some unintelligible film in Serbo-Croat at the N.F.T. and who would bother to give her the business when they got home. 'Are the children asleep? Good, I just wanted to say you look ravishing tonight, darling.' And they would probably vote S.D.P.

She could always be (also, though probably not concurrently) a mistress that he kept in a 'pied-à-terre' style room in Judd Street, and his goodwife and three children (both) rest comfortable, secure and happy in their one-time oasthouse near Ashford, or is it Maidstone? Anyway, God preserve us from goodwives and their children and especially preserve me, Icks (if you're listening, I mean this one), from Goody Icks and her children desire, which will force me into a factory for good, and I'll be taking factories and council flats seriously and look pale and ashen and be forty at my machine, hoping for a break and knowing that I won't get one except by bloody brown-nosing to get made foreman. Fucking foreman! Fuck fore-men and fuck fore-lock tugging and fuck being polite to guvnors who've got oasthouses in Kent and one rooms in Judd Street with a nice young bird in it who wears pink lipstick and is neat minded, bending to crumple her butt while he rearranges his hair into a walnut whip (oh this breeze here), a fucking walnut whip to cover the bald bits and he complains to her as she stands, about the state of the tax system, him not being allowed to claim any tax back off the mortgage on Judd Street and what a hard time he's having, you should hear how that bitch in the oasthouse goes on at me and things are getting worse all the time but I can't do anything because of the children (them again) and he slides his arm around her slender waist and fingers the elastic for her slip and then gets horny when he finds no knicker elastic because no knicker wearing is she. She won't let him down, at least while he's got his American Express card or perhaps she won't let him down anyway and he's much much luckier than he deserves.

Fuck Goody Icks nailing me down in front of a lathe, she's not getting that just to satisfy her maternal instincts, and fuck her going on about it all the time since she's found out she's only got one fallopial or whatever they're bloody called and fuck me too because my head still hurts where that joanna dropped on it or whatever that copper did.

'Elf. Come and sit down.'

And fuck the stupid old paviour wage-slave who let himself get put out of his homeland because of a want of spuds or for blight or whatever it was, and, having got here, dug dug dug his way from Manchester to here before finding himself in London and out of work and changed his trade to start laying stones for his betters to walk on, the men, Victorian, thinking of putting one right up the dewy lipped woman who was neat minded and wore a bustle and stays but kno nickers so she looked all sweet but could have him an 'andful in the back of an 'ansom cab, moving slightly for comfort in her bustled butt. Maybe the paviour was laying stones for his worsters (if there are betters there must be worsters) so that they can sleep on them only temporarily, being moved away by the bluebottles, 'Come along now, move on. And take that piece of card with you.' 'Lift up your bed and walk . . . *cock*' and Elf knew that the copper had always been one with a black beard and mad eyes and would start to call his subject 'scum' if he didn't rouse himself immediately and move on quickly.

'And the river's been here for thousands of years and has seen it all.' He turned to face her. Time flowing past as the river stands still, on and on and on and on and on. Rise and fall tide stationary river, ebb and flow time. Slip like a house-martin under the eaves of experience, but I am not so agile.

'Elf.'

'Yes, I'm sorry. Did you know this was part of the river till the Victorians?'

'No. I've never thought about it.'

'Well it was. And the Strand was a strand, literally that, and Somerset House was built to allow little boats to float in and out and the river was down here watching it all go past, the same river,' he pointed, 'not the same particles of water but the same river. It came here before time and it was here before history for the first men to take their fish. They were free men.'

'But their lives were short.'

'Perhaps. Yes, perhaps their lives were short but they weren't being crushed. They were all equally short lived, like tribesmen in Africa.'

'People aren't better off for being in Africa. That's a silly romantic idea of savages that live in the pink bits on old maps. They all died already of 'flu and syphilis.'

Elf sat beside her, fine face Africa girl, and he shivered suddenly for cold and pulled the jacket apart, putting his arms around her and enjoying her warmth, bringing his nose close to her ear and touching it gently and she squeezed him for a response, yes, tonight isn't a complete write-off, as he could smell the light oil in her hair and feel her brown arm around him, Elf thought he could almost feel the warmth of the brownness and he could sit back and look at her lamp-black eyes.

'Have you been there?'

'No. But my father talked about it and he was disappointed at the way things went after independence. And I suppose I was also, even though I'd never been there.'

'You've never been?'

'No. It would be awkward. My Dad was, what should you say, a political thinker. I wouldn't be welcome.'

'But you're welcome in Vicky Park?'

'This is my home. I'm English. Don't you start that rubbish.'

'I'm not starting, I meant that Clapham's your home, not the other thing. I wondered what you were doing right over in Vicky Park.'

Nancy stood. She walked to the embankment wall, leaning and looking up at Cleopatra's needle until the roar of a passing lorry had faded. She had left the coat with Elf on the seat and she watched as he wrapped it around himself until only his pointed face protruded, fine of lip-slightly-pursed and deep eyes darkened in the sockets by the little light available, short brown hair untidy above.

'I had an appointment over there. What *is* this?'

'Sorry.'

'Well, to save any further complications I'm a hairdresser and I'm freelance, okay. I work in other people's houses, *black* people, which is what takes me to Hackney. Double okay? No more third degree?'

'Sorry.' He stood. 'Here, you'll get a cold'; and he wrapped the coat and himself around the woman and kissed her full on the lips and she kissed him too, beautiful soft giving and he knew of her as he allowed his lips to brush hers. Nancy pushed her lips against him as a promise, which pleased him.

'Take me home,' and Elf nodded and they turned to stroll away, arms about each other and warmth and closeness, pausing only for Elf to aim a kick at the crumpled cigarette. He missed.

They walked back to Blackfriars and could find no taxi so they strolled on into the middle of the bridge and Elf pointed things out to Nancy as if she were a newcomer to the city, finally pointing to the south side and claiming it as a large part of his youth, before he went back to Hackney, untruthfully for it was not the see of Bœrmond, as he said, but Southwark, and Nancy pointed this out so that he had to admit, no, it's not Bermondsey particularly there, I just meant generally the south side. 'It wasn't my real home either. My Mum and Dad were skint so I lived with my grandparents. He worked in the dock, my grandad, and I was very small. I went to Tooley Street when I was little, I expect I was four or five. I'm not sure really why we went now but I remember the street was still cobbled then and it was really early on a winter's morning.'

'Really cobbled? Right up until the fifties?'

'Yes, I'm sure, or nearly sure. Parts of it were cobbled anyway, and the cobbles were wet and it was cold and windy. I remember, this is the *most* thing I remember out of all my life, standing there and watching the men run from dock to dock for work and the clatter of their army boots. They all wore army boots that used to spit and scratch and clack on the cobble stones as they ran.'

'Then there must have been cobbles.'

'I think so. Yes, there must have been.'

'Why did they run?'

'Because they were casuals and they had to stand in groups outside the dock while the foremen chose the ones they wanted. Then if they were out they'd run to the next dock to see if they'd catch the foreman's eye there.'

'Are you sure you remember it?'

'I think so.'

'How awful.' She squeezed him.

'Yes. How awful.' I'm going to be unfaithful again, if my luck holds out. How awful. 'Let's find a cab, Nancy. I've got my car left in Camden but it's not a BMW.'

'What is it?'

'A Triumph.' Elf smiled.

Bethnal Green (Friday)

Chapter Eight

Elf reached his flat at about 7.30 a.m., nodding to the milkman's cheerful, 'Nightshift now then?' and wink.

Carol was sitting in the living room in her dressing gown.

'Where have you been? I've not slept. Were you in trouble? Couldn't you have phoned?'

He sat in a chair opposite her.

'Which one do you want answered?'

'Are you all right?'

'Yes, I'm all right. I got nicked.'

'Oh Elf, what for?'

'It's a long story. I won't end up in court though.'

'Are you sure?'

'Yes. Don't worry.'

She stood and pulled him to her but he resisted.

'Don't.'

'Well what happened?' Carol sat again opposite him.

'It's a long story. I said. Do you *have* to wear a nylon dressing gown?'

She pulled at the gown uncomfortably but said nothing, it's the only one I can afford. I'd better not get him onto that now.

'Is there any breakfast?'

'I'll get some. I've got to get on to work. Couldn't you have phoned?'

'No. And coffee?'

'Yes. And coffee. Did you phone your work?'

'Um, yes.'

'Elf, did you?'

'What about the coffee?'

'*Have* you?'

'No.'

'Oh Alfred! What do you think will happen?'

'Stop worrying.'

'But we owe the electric and the rent. What'll happen if you lose the job?'

'We've been through all that, there's no good in going on now, Carol . . .' he stood, 'you know what would do you, what *would* have done you a good turn? A right good favour? No, you don't but I'll tell you. What would have done you a good favour is, when the sky pilot said, "Does anyone know of any reason why these two shouldn't get right on with it", or whatever it is they say, "speak now or forever 'old yer piece", know what I mean? Someone, one of your bloody useless uncles or your stupid brother, Boil . . .'

'He wasn't there.'

'Well he should've been, he could have made himself useful by shouting out "I do!" after the sky pilot, instead of all of them sitting there like fucking tailor's dummies,' he whirled before her, holding up his hand, '"I do! I know why, mister. Our Carol needs a good plain man, a hard working husband, and it's a well known fact, your reverend, that the Ickses are all good for nothings,"' and Elf slapped the palm of the hand he had held up hard on the surface of the tatty gate-leg table his mother had given them, , '"good for bleeding nothings, and this one's as bad as all the rest of them, probably worse and he'll never hold a job down because he is so bleeding useless!" *Useless*! Me! Good for nothing! Why d'you stick it?'

Carol stood in the doorway between the kitchen and the living room, pulling (still) absently at the front of the nylon dressing gown. She felt profoundly ill at ease with herself and was surprised to find herself the subject of an attack rather than attacking, after all, wasn't it he who'd stayed out all night?

'I've got to get to work.'

'Useless! Don't you hear? We're trapped together in this here and we were useless as a couple to start with and we're getting more useless all the time. We're sinking, Carol, pushing each other's heads down into the bloody mire. Pushing each other's heads down into these poxy jobs . . . look at this place! Look! We're sinking here!'

She went into the kitchen.

'Look at me, Carol.'

'No,' she called back, 'you ought to be careful. You can't unsay everything you say in an argument.'

'It's not an *argument*, that's not the point.'

'One of us has to work, Elf. One of us has to pay the bills.'

'Fuck the bills.'

'Look,' she popped her head around the door, 'I have to go to work. Go on about it tonight if you must. I just don't have time to argue now.'

'It's not a bloody argument. You should be saying these things to me, Carol,' she walked past on her way to the bedroom, 'not me to you. Why don't you go and get yourself a divorce, admit the game's up, get some nice young man and a mortgage on a semi in Hockley. You're young enough and still good looking enough. Still! *You should be saying this to me!*'

'What should I say? That you should get a nice young man and settle down in Hockley? That you're still good looking?' Carol's voice came back from the bedroom, sarcastic and strained slightly as she pulled a dress over her head, 'I'll tell you what, Elf, if I say you're a nice young man will you give me a lift in?'

'I can't. The motor's up in Camden.'

'What's it doing up there?' She came in and leaned across the table, looking into the mirror there on the wall and brushing her hair with short, aggressive strokes.

'It's where I went with Claude.'

'Before you were arrested.'

'They reckon I wasn't arrested. I was asked in to assist with enquiries.'

'Assist with enquiries? Voluntarily?'

'No.'

'I call that an arrest, then.'

'Yeah.' Elf picked up his broken novel from the sofa. 'Yeah.'

'Bye.' She waved at him from the doorway. 'Must rush.'

'Yeah bye.'

And the front door slammed on Elf while he spread the pages of the broken book on the table top like a game of giant patience. Where the hell is number fifteen? Oh I'd better get some sleep or I'll never manage to work.

He went into the bedroom, closed the curtains and lay upon the bed. Outside his window two girls were giggling on their way to work, clip clop high heel, clip clop trip too high heel. Elf couldn't make out clearly what they were saying, probably discussing bloody babies. Now they're closer,

'. . . and then he put his hand there!' giggle giggle giggle, 'and I said,' they stopped for a second so that she could deliver the punch line, 'I said, " 'ere, what sort of girl do you think I am?" and he said, "Go on girl, be a sport." '

'Be a sport! Blimey, out of the ark.'

'Yeah, be a sport.' Giggle giggle.

'Did you stop him?'

'No. He had lovely eyes and lips and he kept on at it, trying.'

'And were you a sport?' Giggle.

'What d'you think?' Giggle giggle. They walked on, clip clop. Elf could hear a baby crying in the next block. The milkman's van whined in the yard. Why's he still here? Been in with someone, dirty bastard. It's true what they say about milkmen. There was a stack of paperbacks on the bedside cabinet and Elf sorted through them, selecting a large and floppy one and placed it open over his eyes. I'd better get some sleep. Be a bleedin' sport. Be a sport, I should say so.

Tottenham Court Road

Chaper Nine

'Two more capuccinos, please, George.'
  ''kay.'
  'I think it should be capuccini, if it's two. I'm not sure.'
  'So what. Just carry on.'
  'Oh . . . there's not that much more to tell.'
  'Tcha! Did you tear Africa woman?'
  Claude nodded thanks to the waiter for the drinks.
  'Speak English. What's tear?'
  And Claude opened and closed his fist slowly, looking directly at Elf.
  'Oh . . . oh no, *course* I never. I went round there for a kip. I'd had a very tiring evening.'
  'What!' screeched Claude, slapping the table top with his hand and his voice rising falsetto. They both fell into laughter, ignoring the stares from the gelateria's other customers. Elf looked round at them, slowly spooning their ice-creams and dipping their heads rather than meet his stare, stare drop then stare again on return, who are these two yobbos? The room was pure fifties Italian; formica tops, chrome chairs and five large, dome-covered neon lights set into the roof. After the daylight it had been like walking into an operating theatre and, looking towards the door, Elf could see the green-hue neon locked in battle (and losing, of course) with the yellower daylight.
  'And a tutti frutti also, me son,' Elf called.
  The waiter turned, frowning, and replied with the merest of nods. The steam from the Gaggia rose directly behind his head, behind his frown even.
  'And then?'
  'And then I'm going to eat it.'

'The Africa woman?'

'You've got a one track mind. She's *English*, anyway, and I am going to eat the ice cream.'

'"And then" for yesterday, I meant.'

'And then I went to work and Old Harry has me in his office, looking over the top of his glasses, and then he says, "Do you know, Alfred, how many times you've been late since you've been here?" and then I guess and he says, "More," and then I shrug and *then*, Claude, he says, "Do you know how many times you've been absent without a sick note?" and I make out to think and then shrug again, and he says, "I think you'd better go up to the wages office and collect your cards, Alfred. We seem to be managing to struggle on quite well without you."'

'And then?'

'And then I went home and got me ear bent for half an hour by Carol.'

'And *then*?'

'And then I said, "Don't you think you're being a little unreasonable? I mean you know my talent's wasted down there," and she started hollerin' and pissed off round her sister for a good bawl. And then I went down the Builder's and got legless and she was there when I got back and starts hollerin' again and I topped out kippin' on the couch.'

'Tough,' said Claude. 'Hard lines.'

'A bit, but it had to come. I'm not that bothered, but I'd better get me hands on some dough soon or I'll be right in it.'

'*You* have! Tcha!'

'What's all this "tcha" business? You sound like a Jamaican washerwoman.'

'And this is all I'll be when they cut off my future. It's hard man dunning me, Elf. *Hard* oo!'

'Who is?'

'The people. Bad men.'

'Who? Do I know them?'

'Don't worry.'

'Who?'

'What's it matter who? What are you going to do, Kung Fu them for me?' Claude smiled and held up his hands, fingers straight and flat and hand circling before Elf's face. 'Too much "Late Night", Elfy boy . . . Ah soo! Kung Fu!' He slapped the hands together. 'Too much "Late Night".'

A teenage girl sitting with her shopping mother behind Claude looked up from her ice cream and smiled at the slap. She had an oval, tanned face and big brown eyes. Elf winked and smiled back, but the girl looked away, picking up some thread from her mother's conversation, 'and so I *said* to her'.

'I don't go to "Late Night". There are too many black boys there getting excited about the film and looking for someone to juk with their blades.'

'Shit. You should come with me,' and he crooned quietly, 'Everybody go Kung Fu fightin', Kung Fu fightin',' stopping suddenly and looking directly at Elf, 'you'd be safe with me.'

'Except if your duns were there.'

'Then . . .' Claude circled his outstretched hands in the air again, chopping quickly at an imagined target, 'we watch the film together, pick up a few hints and pow! Kung Fu! We take them. You an' me.'

'Prick . . . *who* is it?'

'Those guys at the blues.'

'Bright?'

Claude nodded.

'Brilliant.'

Elf stood, stopping the waiter, and paid. They walked out into the yellower light.

'Are you interested in making some money?' Elf raised his voice against the traffic.

'Course.'

A young woman pulled at Elf's arm,

'Personality test?' Her eyes were blue and she was tall, so that the blue eyes looked even into Elf's face and seemed to focus on a point three inches or so behind his nose. Elf looked at her carefully, but the focus didn't change. She wore no make up and her hair was scraped back into a painfully tight bun. 'Would you like to come in and get your personality tested?'

Elf paused. The girl's gaze had dropped to his lips. She must be mutt and jeff.

'Are you joking?'

'No I'm not,' smoothing the smock dress with her hands, 'it doesn't take long. My name's Karen. What's yours?'

'It does not,' Elf smiled, 'take long, and no thanks.'

'But it only takes a minute.'

'Longer than that, Karen my love, longer than a minute. But

99

you're right, it doesn't take long. Bye.' Elf held his hand to his face and waved his fingers at her.

Elf and Claude walked on. Karen forget them immediately and stopped a kindly looking man in a business suit who leaned his middle-aged head to one side as he listened patiently to the pitch. She'd spent many months learning the pitch. She believed herself to be something of a psychologist – through the grace of God, of course. 'Would you like a personality test? It doesn't take long. My name's Karen. What's yours?'

'Money,' prompted Claude.

'Oh . . . yeah. Carol's brother, Boil, reckons he's mobbed up with some hoods. I thought I might ask him to find me something. He has asked me in before. You interested?'

'Yes.'

'Even before you know what it is?'

'Yes. I need it.'

They paused to look at the electronic tricks in a shop doorway, cb base unit £65, hifi speakers £240 (sale . . . bleedin' *sale!*), Tandy tape £200 or more, car radio £80.

'How much you got?'

Claude stuffed his hand into his hip pocket. '£3, and some silver.'

''s that it?'

'Yup, and a cheque coming for yesterday's session. I don't know when that'll come.'

'Signed on?'

Claude nodded. '£45 every second Saturday. If I didn't eat for two years I could pay them.'

Elf pointed at the shop window. 'Ain't got a brick handy?'

'No. Can't afford one.'

'Baby, you *need* the money.'

'I know.'

''s that Bright and his boys still in the nick?'

'Bright was never in the nick. They got his boys but he was first out the door, then sent a smart lawyer down to get his boys.'

'But they must know him.'

'No. He keeps it all at a distance. He's hardly ever there.'

'Have they ever had him?'

'I don't think so. Innocent lookin' Coolie-boy, I don't think they'd know who he was if they got him. You know how innocent Asians look, well, that's Bright. He's got tough boys and uses his head, keeps at a distance.'

'They don't even *know* him?'

'Not as far as I know. What's it to me? I'm not de claat babylon.'

That's Bright, thought Elf, that's bright. He's bright, okay. They turned into an alleyway, a turn away from the crowds and traffic and a turn away from conspicuous consumption-land. You can't even fit a Mercedes in this alley, ancient and cobbled and quiet as it is. Leaning buildings to form it and fresh faced secretaries, last-of-the-summer-sun girls in sharp 'A' line skirts and blue or pink cardys 'excuse-me'-ing past on their way for a cottage cheese sandwich and a bag of crisps at 'Tubbies'.

Soon there were no secretaries and they were alone in the alley, being two hundred years into Defoe land and seeming two hundred miles from Tottenham Court Road, twentieth-century style.

'The young African woman wants some more of that stuff she bought from his boys. You understand?'

'Why can't she ask them?'

'She don't know 'em.'

'She bought one stick off 'em that night.'

'Do you want her money or not?'

'Yes. But she'll have to wait. Streets are pick clean in Norf London an' Brixton too.' Claude leaned against the wall, an already leaning wall so that the angle formed made them both, Claude and wall, look about to fall over. 'That's what they're dunning me for, Elf.'

'I'm not with you.'

Claude pushed a splinter of wood with his shoe. He looked up suddenly.

'There's 'erb due. But it's big, a lot of money, too rich for the blood even of Sir Lord John Bright. He needs to call in all debts, so,' he held up his hands, like a wild west bank job, 'his boys give Claude the runaroun'. "When ya cum up wiv de stuff Claude, claat. Ya owe, bwai, ya *owe*. You *late*. Cum froo, Claudy, or me gonna mash ya. Cum froo."' Claude suddenly grasped his own throat with his right hand, then pulled it free with the left, feigning difficulty and leaving his eyes popping in mock (or not-so-mock) fright. '"Jus' a little. Me mash ya jus' a little."' He pulled up his shirt, crushing the canary yellow cloth in his hands and extending his index finger into his bared belly. A dark bruise stain extended from the ribcage to the waist, a ripple of black and yellow seeping ugly through the brown pigment of his belly.

'Which one?'

Claude shook his head and dropped the shirt, allowing the tail to flap outside his trousers. 'Doesn't matter.'

'It *does*.'

'One, another. You can't take them all on. How much does she want?'

'Dunno. How much is it?'

'Forty. Money up front.'

'I'm seeing her tomorrow. Forty, then.'

'That's so. But she has to wait till it come.'

Elf walked towards a pub on the corner of the alley. 'Come on, I'll buy you a beer and phone Boil,' he turned suddenly to face Claude, his face serious and intense, 'and Claude.'

'What?'

'Tuck your shirt in.' Elf held out a note. 'Mine's an orange juice. I'll get straight on the blower.'

Claude went to the bar while Elf struggled with a phone that didn't work, then left in search of one that did. Though the pub was not crowded, Claude had still not been served when Elf returned.

'Oi! Cloth ears, yeah you. Summink wrong with you?'

'Sorry?' the barman answered.

'You will be, cock. Don't you recognize my china?'

'No.'

'Well you will. He's not a man used to being kept waiting.'

'Oh yeah.'

'Yeah. He don't go for this "wogs last" crap, know what I mean? Neither do I. One orange juice and . . .?'

'One pils,' said Claude.

'I take it you're not all that well travelled?' Elf asked.

'What? Here,' the man opened the drinks, 'er, thirty-four, eighty-eight.'

'Which?'

'Eighty-eight. I was counting.'

'Well don't count on me, me ol' son. Keep the change. Don't blow it all on that travelling.'

They walked to a table.

'He says to bell him later. Reckons he might find something,' Elf chuckled and pointed at the floor, 'right up our alley.'

Claude looked at the floor. 'Here?'

'No . . .' Elf leaned closer, ''s a blag, but there's these other mateys s'posed to be in on it. So he has to talk to them and see what he can do. Still fancy it?'

'What sort of blag?'

Elf shrugged. 'You fit?' He pointed at Claude's belly.

'Yeah . . . I'm fit. You done this before?'

'No.'

'You seem very confident.'

'Wait and see. You shouldn't pin too much on it, it may not happen . . . come on, finish up.'

'Where you going?'

'Park mate. Down the park.' Elf patted his thighs. 'Must keep in some sort of condition . . . coming?'

But Claude shook his head slowly, saying nothing.

Smithfield

Chapter Ten

The maroon Jaguar rolled easily and powerfully along Upper Thames Street. Elf enjoyed the feel of the engine ready to answer every toe touch of the pedal, touch toe, toe touch.

'Watch your speed, Elfy boy.'

The long bonnet reflected white dazzle haze from the sun. They stopped for the lights at Southwark Bridge; red, orange/red, to green but we still can't move, why doesn't anyone take any notice of the yellow boxes?

'There's too much traffic,' said Elf. He held the wheel tightly.

'Come on, calm down.' The man sitting next to Elf raked back his seat as he spoke; as relaxed as he could, to show them; as far as he could, so that he could stretch his long legs under the glove box. He was an ugly man in his mid-thirties, with mean grey eyes peering menacingly around each side of a large nose.

Lance or, as Elf preferred to call him, Boil, was Carol's half-brother, and considered himself to be a man of the world, Jack-the-lad, with money in his pockets and a drum in Hornchurch. He ran around with people who figured (at least in his imagination) as Very Tough Guys. Lance felt, since he ran around with these guys, that he too was a Very Tough Guy. He was pleased with this. He had spent his early years of thieving gathering about himself a collection of Tough Guy Anecdotes. Later still he'd taken a woman, Noleen, who was just weak enough to take slapping around without making too much noise, but just pretty enough and strong enough that he could take her down the Moby or the Volunteer without getting shown up. Lance also had a couple of sub-Tough Guys, to whom he sub-contracted the occasional minor blag and whom he felt (as a consequence) entitled to push around (but less than Noleen, of course).

Lance had also spent his early years of thieving doing just enough bird to make his stories believable.

At home Lance made bad jokes that everybody had to laugh at or face his anger. He favoured silk shirts with rather large collars. He didn't like to have Elf in his house, which suited them both, though he did like to have Carol around because she admired him without being very sure what he did, and offered to make him endless cups of tea and slices of toast when Noleen wasn't around to do it. If only she wouldn't insist on dragging along her husband. Elf made it clear to Boil whenever he drove Carol down that he didn't want to do it and would prefer not to be here. Elf looked at Boil steadily and ignored his tantrums. Once Boil had teased Elf with an offer to come on his 'team' and had been surprised when Elf ignored the offer, not 'Yes' nor 'No' nor 'Who do you think I am?' nor even (and Lance felt this would be the best response) 'Yes *please*, Lance'. His half-sister's husband had just ignored Lance, carried on reading the *Mirror* as if nothing had happened. This had left Lance uncomfortable and unsure and unable (even) to throw a tantrum, so that all that was left to him was to bawl out Noleen for there being no lager in the fridge.

So it was that when Elf had phoned Lance and asked for what he called a 'taster' Lance had taken his chance, agreeing immediately and leaving his subbies more than slightly miffed. Lance didn't care about his subbies. Lance wore a gold bracelet (thick) on his wrist and a gold chain with his name (also in gold) about his neck. Lance believed that he cut quite a figure. He liked to be seen around. Lance was, in short, a prick.

'See, your trouble is, Elfy boy, you get too agitated, know what I mean?'

Elf stared steadily through the screen, a huge yellow bar across the rear of the huge yellow lorry in front announcing 'Long Vehicle' through the plastered-on road dirt. Anyone who thinks it's a Mini shouldn't be driving. What's this clown on about? Shut up Lance. Elf said nothing. With a burst of black diesel oil sweeping across the Jag's bonnet the lorry pulled forward. Elf put his car into gear (his? Possession is nine points of the law, the tenth being 'don't get caught in possession').

'Red,' said Lance, 'stop here.'

Elf dropped the gear lever back into neutral, then pushed the button for the electric window, closing it again quickly as the last of the lorry's exhaust fumes drifted in. He looked at the clock.

'We've got time, though?'

'Agitated.' Lance leaned forward, holding his hand up before Elf's face, palm cupped, fingers slightly apart and pointing upwards. He turned the hand back and forth, a circular motion on the axis of the wrist. 'Agitated, Elfy. I thought you was going to turn out good. I'm disappointed already. I've gone to a lot of trouble Elf, pulled some right stunts to get you in on this. *Personal* trouble.'

'Yeah. All right. Don't do a fucking fan dance.'

Green. They moved forward.

'I want to see how you shape out.'

'Up.'

'Out . . . up. *And* your oppo in the back here. Chocolate drop.'

'He's all right.'

Lance turned in his seat. 'Are you all right, chocolate drop? Have you got bottle?'

Claude may have been asleep, eyes closed and head nodding gently in time with the suppressed lurching of the big car.

'Give it a rest, Lance, eh?' Elf said.

Lance leaned back in his seat.

'Through there,' he said, '*driver*. Once you get up into Smithfield you have to hang a left. I'll say when.'

They passed the back of Saint Paul's and turned in front of the Old Bailey. 'That's it now, drop down to the left again, there, yes there. Just park on here.'

The tyres of the Jag creaked on the kerb and Elf opened the window again.

'Good. Now,' Lance half turned in his seat so that he could address them both. He liked this bit, it was like being an officer before the troops went over the top. He had no fear, he told himself, just a slight apprehension. Over the top. 'Right. There's the alley and he's due in five minutes or so. I know what he looks like, so you, Claude, don't go jumpin' no travel agents goin' for a pint, right?'

'Right.' Claude nodded.

'And *don't* crown him. Watch what I do. Go for his elbows,

knees and bollocks. Smack him in the mouth to shut him up if you have to but it's not the third world war, right? We want his bag. The *bag*. We want the dough. There are no consolation prizes.'

'An' what are you goin' to be at while I'm doin' all this fumpin' an' grabbin'?'

'What d'yer think? *I'm* going to clout him first, so you know we've got the right one. Just do your bit. Keep your nerve and try not to clout him over the bonce . . . and all *you* have to do, Elf, is keep the engine running, don't catch the eye of no coppers and don't get blocked in by no meat lorries. Your bit's a piece of piss.' He smiled. 'I don't know what we're doing paying him out, do you, Claude?'

Claude didn't answer, but Lance wasn't really looking for an answer. He hadn't needed, either, to go over what should or should not happen, they'd done that enough times. It was Lance's act again and he was enjoying himself.

'Gotcher stick and hat?'

'Under the seat,' Claude reached, picking up the axe handle. He stuffed it under his jacket.

'Wish us luck then, Elf,' asked Lance, completely overdoing it at last. Elf sunk forward, leaning his brow on the top of the steering wheel and trying to ignore his brother-in-law.

'Eh . . . Elf?'

He closed his eyes against Lance's persistence.

'You all right Elf?'

'Yes Boil,' Elf looked up, 'I'm all right. Go and do it.'

'Have you got the keys to the other motor?'

'Yes. Go on. Buzz off and do your bit.'

The door clicked, Jaguar quiet, and Elf turned on the radio so that the music played softly, stopping now and becoming soft played speech. He'd expected waiting to be the worst part and now he knew it would be, even at the start of it. Elf watched the backs of the men as they walked towards the alley, a shaft of light at the far end serving to silouhette the figures, tall white and small black, now black and black shadow formed against the light and sometimes shocked by the red of a passing bus or the yellow or blue cast attending a delivery van as it sped past their doorway.

The waiting would be the worst part. Worse than deciding to do it? Elf picked up a flat cap from the dash-top and pulled it on, dragging down the cheesecutter peak to shroud his eyes in shadow. Lorries and vans drove past him, market porters pulled their barrows, snatches of conversation drifted past with the porters and sometimes a call along the street, oioi! all right me son? Well hurry up then! A fat man in a blue suit stood calling to a porter and clutching his clipboard. The porter nodded and waved politely, waiting until the man disappeared into his office before he began to curse.

Elf smiled. Waiting wasn't the worst part; deciding to be a stranger in your own land, amongst your own people, that was the worst part. He leaned back in his seat, pulling at his cap again, and he knew that this even wasn't true, this even wasn't the worst part. You're always a stranger amongst your own, that's the truth. It just becomes clearer now than at other times. All things, don't bullshit, all right then *lots* of things have times when they become clearer, even though they might be there nearly all the time. You're sounding like a class one mystic, Icksy. But it's true, like being frightened or like being in love, when you know that you're staring at eternity and your time is short and it's clearest and you're weakest just when you're feeling strong. The closer you get to women the more frightening it is, because you're more and more at risk and you *know*.

'You know it must end, one way or another,' he whispered, peering from beneath the cheesecutter at a traffic warden on the far side of the street. She walked on, appearing not to have seen him. Perhaps it's tea-time in Snow Hill and she's going to rest her varicosers and dip her beak in a mug.

When in all these years have you been in love then? Elf turned the radio off, wiping the knob carefully with a cloth and pulling on his gloves. I'm not sure what that question means. It's not clear, I'm not frightened enough.

Claude ran from the alleyway. Are you frightened enough now? Is it clear? Elf picked up the cloth and wiped the dash again, nervously. Claude dropped the axe-handle and tore off his balaclava as he ran towards the Jag, a longer stride and then he vaulted a barrowful of meat.

'Hold up!' The barrow-boy staggered, a wobbling, drunken walk as he tried to control his load. Elf put the car into gear and allowed it to ease forward, now gathering speed. Claude was dragging at the front door.

'He's . . .' He fell into the seat, breathing hard and unable to say it. Boil was running past the barrow-boy, skidding past each other on the cobbles and the barrow piled high with carcasses. Now the barrow was bowling downhill, unbalanced, and a comic look of horror was on the porter's face as he desperately tried to hold on. Boil was still wearing his balaclava, strange-looking in the sunshine, and he held a briefcase close to his body. Claude had gathered breath, and he pointed.

'He's mad! *Mad*!'

Claude pulled his swinging door shut, and Boil climbed into the back of the car, laying flat on the seat as Elf accelerated away, finally tipping the white coated barrow-boy under a pile of lamb from his own fallen load as the Jag rushed past.

'Claude!' shouted Boil.

'He's got a bleedin' shooter Elf!' Claude knelt upon the seat so that he could accuse and inform at the same time.

'Claude!' Boil shouted again. He was so stunned by Claude's behaviour that all he could do was repeat it, 'Claude!' until he recovered. Elf didn't speak at all, tight lipped and nervous after narrowly missing the barrow-boy, relieved that there were no police cars in the rear view mirror, swinging the car now wildly north onto Farringdon Street, screech sideways swing in front of the Job Centre ('Come in and choose a job', they should be on the stage with a routine like that; it's funny how fast your brain works when you're frightened and you get plenty of leisure time to examine the things around you, power on now, turn it all on . . .) and they race past the queueing traffic, right past the 'keep left' sign.

'Slow down. No one's after us,' from Boil, levering apart the black attaché-case as he spoke and ignoring Claude still kneeling over him from the front seat and glaring.

'Are you tooled up?' asked Elf. No reply. 'Where is it?'

'Under me coat. *Do* leave it out you two. Stop here.' They stopped. 'Right you, out. Get the tube.' To Claude.

'Fuck off. You never said you had no shooter.'

Boil screwed up his face and climbed out of the car. They ran through an alley into Saffron Lane and tore two parking tickets off the screen of the Cortina one of Boil's subbies had left for them half an hour since; driving sedately now and heading north again, this time out of Clerkenwell and with Lance on the back seat counting their take, check the mirror again and there's no problems, drive easy to Euston and take the tube.

'Euston?'
'Euston . . . and then the tube. Don't stop too near to it.'
'How much?'
'Not a lot, son.'
'How much?'
' 'bout five hundred each, time we take out expenses.'
'Did you use that?' Elf indicated under Lance's coat.
'Course not.'
'He's mad.' Claude leaned his cold-sweating face near to Elf. 'Barmy. He never said nothing about no shooters,' turning away suddenly and violently, 'you didn't Lance, you bloody never. What would've happened if he'd fought?'
'Shut up.'
Claude shut up, tight lipped with anger. Elf ran his gloved hand across his brow, sweat on the leather and I'm just as frightened as he is, just don't feel it. He pulled in to let a police car pass, blue light flashing headlamps, no siren, heading south. Elf was surprised that he felt no fear even as the police car passed, though he had seen his own wiped sweat on the glove back and he knew he must be frightened.
'He's right Lance. You should've said.'
And now Lance shut up, smiling softly to himself. He pushed the attaché-case under the passenger seat and stuffed the money into his coat. 'Euston,' he said, loudly, and laughed.

Chapter Eleven

Though he had had doubts about Claude's reliability, Boil involved both Elf and Claude in a series of minor blags, none of which netted much more than a few hundred pounds for each man, though, of course, every blag appeared in Boil's mind as being 'maybe the big one', 'the breakthrough' for his team. The breakthrough never came and they never made any *real* money. As Elf noted, the sum of their achievement so far was to develop some expensive tastes and keep themselves rather well.

'But I haven't got a pot to piss in, Lance, really, and every time we go out on one of these stunts we're staring ten years porridge straight in the mush. I don't think the sums work out.'

Boil had trodden this path himself, and he told Elf about 'all you ever do is sweat buckets to earn a little bit, a little bit of rubbish, son'. Boil knew it took bottle to ride out the ponkey ones, stay in there, know what I mean, Elf? Elf did indeed know and nodded an insincere agreement. He was making a mental list of their failures.

There was, for instance, the Great Leytonstone Bookie's Hold Up, and this is the way it always figured in Elf's mind, if not lit in neon, then at least writ in large letters. This blag involved three stolen cars, various weapons and Boil's two subbies as well as Claude, Elf and the great man himself. One of Boil's 'bits of spare', a charming but plain-looking young woman living in a flat overlooking Leytonstone tube was drawn in so that they could use her flat as a 'flop'.

Boil loved it. His own team, and using their brains, not like the apes he'd been forced to hang around with over the past few years. He'd developed an ingenious and elaborate plan which had involved holding up the solicitor's office opposite the bookie's at the same time as the bookie's itself. Since the solicitor's office held no more than £25 in mixed denomination notes and a clutch of mixed 12p and 15½p stamps, the typists (the boss hadn't arrived yet) were somewhat surprised to get the 'hands up!' treatment from one of Boil's subbies (the other was outside as a driver). The subby burst in all flailing blue donkey jacket, sawn-off shooter and stocking mask. It was nine-fifteen a.m. and the typists were only just now settled behind their desks, uncovering the machines, putting their faces on and discussing the film last night on the box.

'He was lovely in it Joyce, *really* lovely . . . I said to my George when we were watching, "Inny *lovely* George?" but he was akip in the chair . . . well, it's his job, he does work hard . . .' The door opens. ' 'ere! What's all this? Whatd'y'want?' she cries.

Gruff voice. 'No sweat ladies. Put yer 'ands up, that's all.'

'We ain't got nuffing!'

The typists put their hands up, a surly girl clicking closed her compact before doing so.

This had all taken place because Boil had calculated on his 'recce' that the typists would be able to see into the bookie's from their office window.

The typists' surprise was as nothing to Boil's own when he scaled the bookie's counter and opened the till.

'What's this?' Boil screamed, turning to the blue-suited young man standing by his side. In his angry scream Boil had spat against the inside of his stocking mask. Now spittle dribbled down his chin, weaving in and out of the nylon.

The betting shop manager swallowed hard.

' 'sall we've got mate.'

'*Leave* off!' Boil picked up his pistol from beside the till and Elf saw a gloved thumb moving over the safety.

'All. 's truth. We banked up yesterday.' The manager of the betting shop was shaking, his face white and the white collar below looking too large, much too large, a big, sweat-covered, white-poplin horse's collar. Elf thought he could almost smell the man's fear. Smell it madam? I'm sitting in it. Boil scooped the notes from the till. He raised the pistol and the notes to the manager's face, pistol one cheek, notes the other.

'You're fucking me about.'

'No mate . . . no.'

'You're on a wind up, ain't you?'

The man shook his head.

'No . . . straight.'

Boil's lips spread behind the stocking mask.

'Straight . . . you lot don't know what "straight" means. Where is it?'

This time the man couldn't speak, his mouth opening and closing as if he were an oversized, Corfam-shod rising trout on a hot summer's day. The till girl looked about to swoon. Claude stood by the door, behind Elf. Claude's head was encased in one half of a pair of black nylon tights. This made his face impenetrable, and his head was like nothing so much as Thursday evening washed and now paired socks, toes tucked within each other. Now the pair of socks bobbed up and down in agitation, and Claude pushed open the door a couple of inches.

'C'mon. Time's up.'

Boil nodded and touched the betting shop manager's nose with his gun, smiling behind the nylon mask.

'Your lucky day son.'

And he followed Claude and Elf out, clasping the few notes.

Another attempt was the Aborted Supermarket Stunt, where Boil had a 'whisper' and they'd spent three days planning their job only to watch a police car double-park next to the security van at the vital moment. The passenger strolled over to a tobacconist's. Elf, Claude and Boil gave up, and Elf began to feel that the signs did not augur.

Despite the mishaps that Elf listed to himself, they did make money, as it is possible to make money, or at least a little money and irregularly at that, but never the sort of money you could make from real thieving, like being a lawyer or an accountant or a banker, and it was never the long term money and never regular.

'What we should do is open a bank,' Elf said, leaning on the pub table, elbows either side of his tomato juice and palms flat against his cheeks, to support his head. Claude was sitting with his shoulder half-turned away from Boil, which Claude felt was only the right attitude to the man. Let him know you're giving nothing away. Boil lifted his palms up.

'All that's good business . . . but if you two want to make a few bob while you're setting it up there's a man I know who wants the screws turned on some matey in Peckham. There's a pony each in it for you . . . just go down and give him the willies, know what I mean?'

They ignored him.

'As I said, it's a pony each.'

Claude stood suddenly and angrily. He raised himself up to his full height and pointed to his head. 'You want me to give the willies . . . me? *ME*?'

People were turning in response to the sound and the barmaid frowned a little at his raised voice, then smiled as he went on, 'Oo am I s'posed to frighten, then? Eh? *Look* at me. I'm . . . five feet four. Look at me muscles . . . oo they s'posed to frighten . . . obeah?'

A big fat pig of a man wearing a strained grey flannel uniform laughed, crack sudden false rising laugh, dry riser under the arch, a piss-taker's laugh, and he turned again at the bar to sup on his Grotney's Fizzo, Falsely Called Beer. Elf felt his anger rising for a second but Claude continued, now a fierce whisper leaning and looking into Boil's face.

'It's *stupid*. Big risks for nothing. Stupid.'

Claude turned on his heel and strode away.

'Where you going?' Boil called.

'Pony.' And he pushed the loo door open.

Elf grinned, then was serious. 'He was right. It's not working out all that well, Lance.'

'That's luck. You have to take the rough with the smooth in this life. It's how things are.' Boil looked up and smiled at the barmaid. She dredged up some coyness from a forgotten corner of her soul and smiled back.

'See . . . there's smooth for you.'

'No. I'm serious. He's got to find a lot of dough, y'know.'

'His problem. You shouldn't get involved with the lazy sods, Icksy.'

'Well, whatever. I don't think we're making any progress.'

Boil stood. 'See if you can come up with anything better. I'm doing him a favour having him around. He's got no bottle and he's got no brains. Drink?'

Elf drained his tomato juice from the glass and held it up to Lance.

'I may,' he said, 'be able to think of something where we could all do a bit and no sweat. If you're interested, Lance. No strain.'

'No strain?' He rapped the table. 'There's always strain, like your mate is having trouble straining his greens. I'll get the drink and you think.' Boil went to the bar. How smooth would the barmaid be? She smiled and Boil thought 'enough', smiling back.

'Pint?' he called to the ceiling.

'No,' Elf called, shaking his head at the man's back, 'another tomato juice.'

Elf didn't want a tomato juice and thought he should leave soon, which was how he always felt in pubs. He waited patiently for Boil to finish pitching at the barmaid. She was ugly enough when she laughed and something Boil said had made her and the man in the rancid grey flannel laugh. Good luck to them. I only have to stand him a little longer if this works. Claude left the loo and began to study the juke-box in great detail. Elf wished Claude would come over and talk, but he could see his friend was angry from the way he was standing, even. Elf thought his idea would work if he could sell it to Boil. If he could get it right. It was a lot to get right, though.

Chapter Twelve

Elf met Nancy in a pub in Clerkenwell Green. She'd wanted it to be outside St Bart's, under the plaque for Wallace, which would have been convenient for her appointment. Elf had refused, without telling her why. The events of three weeks before in Smithfield were too close, and he didn't want to stand around for half an hour for fear of being recognized. This was over-careful but Elf felt over-careful and had insisted that he wait for her in the Clerkenwell pub.

They'd taken one drink only before strolling across Mount Pleasant and through the squares and gardens of the eastern part of Bloomsbury.

'Cromwell's granddaughter is buried here and there's a herb garden behind for blind people, look there's braille signs.'

'Yes. It's nice,' Nancy replied. 'Let's sit for a while.'

They settled on the bench, a green and pleasant lawn and ancient trees before them.

'There's a load of rhododendron bushes down there. It's a great display in spring.'

'How do you know it, Elf?' She took his arm and settled back in the seat. Elf smiled and rubbed the dust off his shoes with his fingertips. 'I used to wander about a lot when I was a kid, during the school holidays and that.'

'Were you lonely?'

'Are you?'

Now Nancy laughed, lightly. A man in a long dark coat on the far side of the gardens stopped, attracted by the sound. He stared at them for a second or two, a sombre figure under the trees and his dark hollowed eyes and pale skin concentrating their attention. He moved on.

'Like laughing in a library,' Nancy said, shivering suddenly. 'You've got new shoes.'

'Yes. I got hold of a few quid . . . don't look like that, it wasn't yours.'

'I didn't suggest you had. It's awful to say that, Elf. I wasn't suggesting anything. It's really awful.'

'Sorry.'

'You have no job yet?'

Don't *you* start.

'No. I did some work for a geezer a couple of weeks ago. He just paid me out.'

'What sort of work?'

'This and that. Paid well.'

'And you're managing?'

'Yes, I'm managing fine. Borage there,' he nodded, 'and fennel.'

'How's Claude?'

'Oh . . . your stuff again. We'll have it soon. We've got something going down, so we'll get it then.'

'Don't worry about it too much. I'm not that bothered . . . what sort of thing "going down"?'

'Well,' Elf leaned back too so that his head was near to her, 'we've found a way to get him off the hook with Bright.'

'Bright?'

'The money. Claude owed it to him and Bright was giving him some stick. He needed it to do some big deal. What we've done is arranged some interest from a geezer, a bit of a hood that I know.' A bit of a Boil that I know. Something of a pimple, really.

Nancy stood and began to walk away.

'Do you want to hear?'

'Yes.' She stopped, frowning and waiting for him.

'You look unhappy. I've got to earn a living somewhere and I'm trying to get my mate, clog-head, out of stuck.'

'I know,' she smiled and linked arms with him again as he came up, 'I've got something on my mind. I'm sorry. Go on.'

'So Bright gets the use of money when he needs it, this hood gets a couple of grand's worth of dope to deal with and Claude gets some more time to pay up.'

'What do you get?'

'I get shot of a lot of problems at once.'

'Isn't it dangerous to get involved?'

'I hope not. I'm not carrying or holding any money or stuff. I'm just arranging it. It'll be over soon.'

They strolled towards the park gates. Nancy appeared to be very apprehensive, and Elf could see this and find no way to relieve it. He said, 'It's tonight, actually, so I'll have to buzz off earlier than usual.'

'At the blues?'

'No. Too dodgy by half. Camden Lock.'

'And you'll be there? Isn't it dangerous?'

'No. I'll just show this hood, Lance, where exactly and then buzz off. Him and his boys can sort out their own business with Bright.'

'Will he be there?'

'Who knows? His boys will. And the stuff. That's why I'm buggering off, I ain't getting caught holding two thousand quid's worth of herb.'

'Don't get involved, Elf.'

'I won't.'

'Don't.' Nancy looked long and directly into his eyes. They stopped. They were standing by the gate and Elf could suddenly hear the traffic passing outside, as if it had never been there. As if they had been in a country garden. He turned and looked back across the little park.

'I *am* involved. And Claude is.'

Nancy walked over to a green painted bench. She folded her hands together, turning them this way and that and finally looking up to Elf.

'Let's sit quietly for a while.'

Elf sat beside her, and as soon as he was settled Nancy said, 'I'm pregnant. I'm afraid, Elf. That's what I was at Bart's for. I was finding out for sure.'

'Oh. Can't you just do it through the post?'

'God knows. I had two goes with kits from chemist's but I got the first one completely wrong and the second one said I wasn't but I'm never late or anything and I knew there was something so I got an appointment there.'

'There?'

'Bart's. Aren't you following?'

'I'm following, it's just a lot to take in all at once.'

'Yes.'

Elf shrugged. You are, you ain't.

'How can it say you aren't when you are? Are you sure?'

'They just can.'

'Oh.' He put his arm around her, but she just looked away. 'It *is* yours, you know.'

'Yes. I'm sorry. I don't mean to behave bad, it's just a shock. I'm trying to get me thoughts together.' He squeezed Nancy's shoulders but she wouldn't look back. 'I'm just surprised, Nancy.'

'Well I'm surprised too.'

'I bet you are. Doesn't seem fair, does it? I mean, there we are, having a laugh and hurting no one and bang, that's it. Am I supposed to say I love you or something?'

'Don't be stupid. What'll you say to your wife?'

'What wife?' Elf sat back from her and glaring.

'Don't. It's not the time to play games. You've never offered me a phone number and you've never asked me to your house. I wasn't born yesterday.'

'No.' Are you a bleedin' witch doctor's daughter? 'Anyway she's left, so I don't have to explain nothing to her.'

The sky grew dark suddenly as a cloud obscured the sun.

'There's no sun now.'

'It's October . . . what do you expect?'

'Yes. It seems sad there's no sun though.'

'It is. There's always spring to come.' Elf was more relaxed now that he had been forced to admit how things really were. How are they? He didn't know, but he knew it was better that things were in the open, just as he knew he didn't want any children to worry about and he couldn't take up another wife even as he was managing to struggle free of one mutually oppressive relationship. He wished he could harden his heart against it. Maybe he could. Maybe he'd ask her if she wanted to marry Carol, that'd work out best all round.

'When did she leave?' Nancy asked.

'Some weeks. Don't let's go on about it all. It's bloody tough luck about you. How d'you feel?'

'I don't know. I'd never thought about it.'

'Look at that cloud.' He didn't want it to go on. 'Will you go right through with it?'

'Yes. I think so. I always knew about your wife. It's easy to tell.' She pulled Elf's arm about her shoulders again.

'Did you not think of, er, prevention?'

'Did you?'

'I thought everyone was on the pill.'

'Well only if it's worth it Elf. I didn't mean to get involved with you. I wasn't expecting to.' She looked about to cry and he did not pursue the matter; besides, he knew she was right, only he found himself saying the words without quite having control over it.

'You'd better have me phone number then.' He began to search through his jacket pockets for a pencil.

'Yes, not now, though. Give it to me later.'

'There won't be no trouble, you know, on the blower and all that. It's straight up . . . I'm on me jack. Have you got a pencil, Nancy?'

'No. I don't know that I want to get any further involved.'

'With me?'

She nodded. 'Let's be quiet now, though. It's nice here and you'll have to go soon.'

'Not that soon.'

'Let's be quiet.'

Elf stopped sorting through his pockets. He watched her face, but soon Nancy closed her eyes and shut him out. Elf found his attention drawn, stupidly and uselessly, to the traffic beyond the gate. He had thought he was beginning to see himself clearly – before this afternoon, that was. Seeing clearly is half of it, he thought, and you can solve things, except if someone changes all the rules, like 'I'm in the puddin' club, Elfy boy'. Choice!

He concentrated very hard on sitting quietly as Nancy had asked, but it wasn't easy. He felt as if he were in a room waiting for something to happen, and that he was watching the park through a long, broad window on the south side of the room. He wanted to stand and pace the floorboards. The dark cloud moved away suddenly from the sun, but the light was no warmer.

Chapter Thirteen

P.C. Higgins was pleased with himself. Before his transfer to the Met he had been sniffing around a woman detective in his old nick. The relationship had been awkward. She was a woman in her mid-twenties, middle height, mid-brown hair and a keen, distrustful, woman detective's face. Higgins saw her as possessing a fine chin and fine blue eyes. 'Wonderful eyes,' he'd told her once. He had believed on this occasion that he loved her. She had shrugged merely when he'd told her.

Anne, the woman detective, drove a big old Rover 80 that her father had given her. She seemed to Higgins to be a wonderfully calm and balanced person, and this calmness had explained the shrug, at least to Higgins' satisfaction. Anne had always been somewhat reserved in their relationship, to the extent that, during their more intimate moments, she kept her teeth firmly clamped together, making him run his tongue (frustratedly) over the teeth but never penetrating to the pink wet warmness he knew would lie behind.

She had excused this to him once by saying that if a girl would do *that* then she would do the other part, but, being encouraged by the fact that she'd once allowed him to put his fingers under her bra straps (never inside the bra proper – though once his fingers had briefly brushed the gossamer outside of one of the cups) he'd persisted anyway, going on to say what a fine chin and wonderful fine blue eyes she had. And Anne had shrugged. Higgins said he loved her, but she didn't answer, simply shrugging a little less expressively.

'What are we doing Thursday?' he'd said, the next time he'd phoned her.

'I don't know what *you're* doing, David. I'm busy.' Click. So there, David. And he'd put down the phone, frustrated. Click.

In their clinches she sometimes smelled slightly tangy of slightly old and slightly acrid sweat. Nylon underclothes sweat. This had only ever served to excite Higgins further, and he could not help recalling the faint tang and her polished mint teeth and wetness as he'd put the phone down. Where was she going? Who could she be going with? 'I don't know what *you're* doing, David.' So there. Click.

Anne had reacted in the same way when he'd said that he was joining the Met.

'I'm transferring to the Met, Anne.'

'The Met?'

'Yes. The Metropolitan Police. I put in for it ages ago. I'm going next week. I've heard.'

'Why would you want to do that?'

No edge in the voice. Just a plain, even, enquiring tone, like 'why did you buy blue curtains' or something.

'I just want to. I think it will be more interesting.'

'Do you want more tea, David?'

'No.'

'It's my round. Have one.'

'No thanks.'

'I'll see you later, then,' and she'd left him in the canteen, smiling to a pretend wolf-whistle from one of the yobs on Traffic who wore long sideburns. They're not even s'posed to come in here for their break, Higgins thought. He went to the serving hatch and bought a tea that he didn't want, stirring in two lumps of sugar that he didn't like. He walked determinedly back to his seat. Dirty bastard bigheads on Traffic.

'D'you know your Rover's got a flat, mate?' he called, but big sideburns smiled and turned his back to Higgins.

David Higgins was pleased with himself. The business of being in the Met had gone so badly that he was determined to do something, 'break the mould' he told himself, a phrase fresh from the leader columns of the *Daily Mail*, perhaps stale from those same columns. David had mentally clenched his fists, and took heart to phone Anne.

'Fancy coming down for a few days, then, well a couple? Show you round the old metropolis? Eh?' and she'd said, 'Yes.' David Higgins was *very* pleased with himself, and not a little

125

surprised. 'A couple of days' meant at least one night, and one night meant . . . well, you never know, you just never know, David. He smiled inwardly. You never know your luck.

Today was the first day and he'd shown her the fleshpots, which seemed to leave her unmoved. David Higgins hadn't questioned that, Soho is quiet at lunch time. He'd taken her northwards, King's Cross way, and, after they'd left the King's Cross pub (for a stroll, you know) the magic teeth had parted for a second to allow the taking of a swift and swiftly ended coition with the woman's tongue, which was pleasure itself to David, even if the tongue carried a taste of tobacco tar too, and David Higgins wished as he touched and tasted it, oh so hot and darting, that he had also taken tobacco. He didn't like tobacco and he couldn't help that he hadn't taken any.

He put his arm around Anne's waist, feeling her not over-slim midriff and occasionally wandering up to the lower 'bones' of her full-length brassiere. He was excited again and walked awkwardly (lest anyone should see) until it went away. But it takes so long to go away and this time it wouldn't, and eventually he began to walk straight again in response to some comment of hers.

'I'll make up a bed in my front room. You can have the divan and I'll have that,' he said, squeezing her again and hoping it surely wouldn't come to that.

'Oh I wouldn't bother with that. I'm going to see someone in South London. Catford, d'you know it?'

'Er, not really. Vaguely . . . girlfriend, is it?'

'No . . . a fellow from there. He was attached to the Regional Crime Squad up at home for a while.'

'So you'll stay there?'

'Yes.' Anne smiled. They were walking south on Judd Street and they turned into Handel Street, pausing in front of the iron gates to St George's Fields.

'I'm thinking of leaving,' he said.

'What, now?'

'No. The job. I'm thinking of leaving the job.'

'Why?'

'I don't like it. It stinks.'

'What else could you do? Have you got any O-levels and things?'

'No.'

The park behind the gates looked enticing, though a grey cloud hovered near. He released her.

'Do you want to go in, David?'

'Yes. It may rain, though. I can see a shelter.'

'It won't.'

'I can see a loo. I'll go in for that at least. I shouldn't have had that last pint.'

'Have you put your ticket in?'

'No. I'll do it as soon as I go back to work.'

Anne took his arm and held it gently. They walked through the gate and David saw Hicks and Nancy. He turned quickly to walk away, but Anne firmed her grip. Elf looked up.

'Oh shit,' he said, under his breath.

'What?' Nancy followed the direction of his gaze.

'Do they know you?' Anne asked.

'Sort of . . . I nicked him.'

'Do you know her?'

'I've seen her.'

He pulled away again, but Anne walked forward. David was forced to follow.

'Hullo, Hicks.'

'Hullo.'

'Nice day, for October.'

'It was. It looks like rain now.' Elf stood and walked past them to the gate and out. Nancy followed, careful not to look into their faces. Anne stared. She walked forward and sat on their newly-vacated bench. She was alone now in the park with David.

'Do you know her?' she asked again.

'I said so. I saw her with him once.'

'Where?'

'What does it matter?'

'I've seen her.'

David sat too.

'Where?'

'Harwich. She's a bit of a linguist, so I saw her there.'

'What do you mean, "a bit of a linguist"? What was she doing?'

'She was in the Customs Waterguard, David. Is he a villain?'

But he did not reply. He thought of the awkward conversations at Peter Street when he'd nicked Elf. The rotten bastards.

'I'd better be off, Anne. I've got to make a phone call.' The rotten swine. Why wouldn't anyone say anything to me? Let me be a right . . . he stood. 'I'm off then.'

Anne was surprised. It was the first time that she'd seen him look so positive. Anne liked it, he always was such a drip until now. Perhaps she'd give Catford a miss after all. She'd only arranged it because she'd thought David was going to be as boring as he usually was. Catford had a beard anyway and she didn't really like beards.

'Will I see you later?'

'I dunno. Phone up tomorrow and see.' He walked away without looking back.

Grand Union Canal (Regent's Canal)

Chapter Fourteen

'Make yourself a cup of tea,' Elf said as soon as he opened the door.

Claude stepped past him. 'Coo, ain't you got an 'oover?'

'I'm busy.'

'Carol was never too busy.'

'Carol ain't here.'

'You don't say.' Claude surveyed the kitchen. It was a mess, pile on pile of unwashed crocks. 'Which cups shall I wash up?'

'Whatever you fancy . . . there's some cheese in the fridge.'

'I ain't,' the West Indian English popped his head around the door, 'opening your fridge. There might be bats in it.' He grinned.

'There is, bat soup. Speciality of the house. I have it as part of my fitness regime.'

'Is that what drove her out?' Disembodied voice from the kitchen. 'Carol.'

'Look, there's nothing wrong with this place, just the washing up.'

'And the ironing.'

'Not much. I don't use much.'

'Have you asked her back yet?'

'No chance. I phoned her but she wouldn't talk. I wasn't asking her to come back but I didn't get a chance to say bugger all.' He leaned back in his armchair and picked up a paperback. He's right. This place is a mess. The phone rang.

''lo.'

'Call me back.'

'Who is it?'

'Who d'you think? Use a phone box.'

'Look love, I've just been reading *The Third Man* too. What d'you want?'

'I'm serious. Use a phone box. Call me. Do it now.'

She rang off.

'Who's that?' Claude came in with two steaming cups of tea.

'Nancy.'

'And?' He set the cups down. 'Milk?'

'No time.' Elf stood, 'she wants us to call her back.'

'Go on then.'

'From a phone box . . . I'm not sure what it's all about but she sounds rough.'

'Melodrama and women,' Claude sipped his tea and sat, 'call her from here.'

'No. She sounded serious. P'raps she's been nicked.'

'Then she'd phone you from a box. She doesn't do anything wrong either. She hasn't even got her dope yet.'

Sip again. Claude had washed up for this tea and he wasn't letting go of it so easily. Elf picked up his car keys.

'Come on. We'll go down Old Street. There's bound to be a blower working down there.'

'Old Street!' Claude stood, controlling the slopping of his nearly full cup with an exaggerated bending of his body forwards and a jerk of the wrist.

'All the ones round here get done over . . . by little black hooligans.'

'And white.' Claude was laughing, and he picked up his jacket again.

'All right, and white. But it's black ones I see doing it.'

They reached the door and Elf held it open, gruesome green council paint on the outside now revealed, lardy pieces of rubbish along the landing, spread evenly. Claude stopped close to him, and they stared together at the ugliness of the landing and at the ugliness of the lard spread and half eaten dry crusts between. Cars in various stages of dismemberment were spread unevenly though always lardily about the yard below them. The council hadn't managed to sweep the yard or wash the communal windows for months. Thank you council, who blame Heseltine. Thank you Heseltine too, but whoever's to blame the yard's still full of shit unswept and the communal windows are covered in dirt, and the cars making it look like a party of dids were camped out below them.

'I have the same trouble with white kids. I can never tell the difference between them, so I'm never sure who broke the phone boxes.'

Elf nodded at the yard.

'Who blames them?'

He closed the door.

They drove to Old Street tube through the twilight melting to darkness, and though it was a short drive, by the time they arrived the cars were lurching red tail-lamps and swinging, staring headlamps, pedestrians white beam-lit. It began to drizzle.

'What's it all about?' Elf held his face as far from the mouthpiece as he could. It stank, as did the subway they were standing in.

'I thought you wouldn't phone.'

'Well I have, Nancy. What's up?'

There was a silence. Elf could almost hear her swallow.

'I'm going to Africa.'

'And?'

'Tomorrow. I may even go to France tonight and go from there.'

''s a bit quick, innit?'

'Don't go tonight, Elf.'

'What?'

'Don't go.'

'Have you done something, Nancy? Have you been indiscreet?'

Oh yes, Nancy thought, I was indiscreet with you. How indiscreet could I have been?

'I'm not a hairdresser, Elf.'

'Oh yeah.'

'Yes. I love you.' Nancy choked and couldn't speak for a second. 'I was supposed to get through to your friend, but it happened with you and I got involved with you.'

'You did that all right. You've fucked us right up.'

'I didn't mean to. I have to go. Don't go tonight.'

'I won't. I s'pose the old bill are going to be there.'

'Yes. I won't see you any more. I'm going to go now.'

'Bye.' He hung up. Elf threw the car keys to Claude. 'Go to my flat and stay there. Do you know how to get hold of Bright?'

'No. What's happening?'

'That Nancy was having us . . . *me* on. The police are going to be at Camden tonight.'

'Oh shit.'

'Yes. Go to the flat and stay there. I'll see if I can clean things up here a bit. I'll see if I can call off Boil at least,' said Elf. Claude stared at him for a second.

'What a cow!'

Elf didn't answer and Elf didn't want to. He turned his back and Claude ran back down the tunnel. What a cow? I don't think so, poor cow, milch cow with my child being due. I wonder if she'll have it now? She must be in a right six and eight. Poor cow.

He rang Carol. 'Your brother there?'

'No. What do you want with my brother?'

'I want to talk to him. Are you all right?'

'Yes. I didn't want to talk to you. Lance is at his friend's house. I'll give you the number.' She found the number and read it to him. 'I thought you were phoning to ask me to come back for a second.'

'Why?'

'I just thought you'd like to try.'

'No . . . why d'you think it?'

'Because you rang. You've only rung once before.'

'No. I didn't ring for that. How's Hornchurch hit you?'

''s nice. It's clean. Ever so clean. It's a long way to work, though.'

'And Noleen?'

'Oh, you know how they are.'

'Yeah. I've got to go. Me money'll run out.'

'Why aren't you at home? Are you in trouble?'

'A bit.'

'Don't get Lance involved in any trouble, Elfy.'

Don't make me laugh. 'No. I won't.' That's for sure (I hope).

He rang Lance and put him off without saying too much. Such was Lance's addiction to being a telly criminal and super secrecy that his only comment was to express some worry about his money. It'll be all right, Lance. Okay, be good, and if you can't be good, Elf. Yes, I know, be careful. Did you think that one up? He put the phone down before Lance could reply.

'O'Keefe, please, C.I.D.'

''d'line please.' A buzz. Repeated. Another voice. 'C.I.D.'

'O'Keefe please.'
'Not here sir. Can I help?'
'No. D'you know where I can get hold of him?'
'He's at home.'
'Have you got the number? It's important.'
'Give me yours. I'll see if I can get him to phone you, what's your name?'
'Elf. It's a coin box, hang on . . .' Elf bent to peer at the number. He read it out to the policeman.
'Hang about then. I'll see what I can do.'
Hang about. The telephones were mounted along the subway wall without sound booths, so that Elf had to listen to a skinhead crooning sweet nothings to his girlfriend while he waited, '*Course* I love you . . . yeah course. I said.' A silence while she croons back, then he begins again, snapping at his yellow braces and leaning his near-shaven head to one side as she speaks, 'I *said* . . . nah, it diddun mean nuffing. You *know* I do.' He began to rub his neck with his free hand, the palm slipping nervously up and down between the neck and the bristle above.

Elf's phone rang.
'O'Keefe.'
'I should bleedin' think so. What sort of fuckin' stunt you been pullin' on us?'
'Don't swear at me, boy. What are you talking about?'
O'Keefe had made the call from his front room, and he could hear the softened murmurs of his children drifting out from the dining room. His wife shushed them, 'Go upstairs for a while, darlings, Daddy's very busy,' and came in to settle in an armchair before him and smile at him. O'Keefe was half listening to Elf. Of course he knew what Elf was talking about, he'd had a similarly bad tempered conversation with a young uniformed boy earlier, and this had entailed much swearing so that he'd said to the boy, 'If you don't mind your manners, son, I'll put you on a charge.' 'Bollocks,' the reply had come back, 'I'm off anyway. You bastards down here all think you're so bleeding superior,' and Higgins had rung off, sweating for fear and sweating for temper. There was no going back now.

O'Keefe had discovered, by a roundabout route involving the calling in of old debts for information at N.S.Y., that the

Customs people and the Drugs squad had been working on his patch without telling him. He was not pleased. O'Keefe's governor hadn't know either, and he was even less pleased. This man had immediately settled down to write letters and memoranda by the dozen on the matter. O'Keefe had closed the door quietly as he'd left, the governor's bald head bent over his papers and shining in the glow of the desk lamp.

'Is it big?' he said suddenly, interrupting Elf.

'No. Couple of grand, that's all.'

'I didn't know about it.'

'I don't care. If I get me collar felt I'm gonna give it all that about you lot that night, fiddling the books and that.'

'Don't threaten me.' His wife looked up, and O'Keefe swivelled so that his back was to her. There was a soft thudding as a child ran across the room above. 'You're not even in the book at Peter Street. There's no collator's card, you're not in that boy's pocket book, what's-his-name. Nobody has ever arrested you in Peter Street. If your involvement is only what you say it is, don't worry. If the other lot nicked you they'd never make it stick. If they brought the girl to court she'd look like a *provocateur*, her evidence isn't worth a monkey's. All they're going to get is a car full of wogs and two grand's worth of hashish . . . big deal. Go to a pub where people know you, preferably one used by magistrates and judges, and make sure you're there with a half pint in your hand while it's all going on. Make sure your mate, whoever, is obvious too. Make sure you're not within miles of it . . . where is it happening?'

'Don't you know?'

'No. Where?'

'Camden Lock.'

'When?'

'Can't say. This geezer was s'posed to sit there tonight until they turned out. On a bench just past the bridge. Did you really not know?'

'I'm afraid it's true. Think about it . . . I'd hardly chat you up if I was trying to nick you, would I?'

'No.' Though Elf didn't feel convinced.

'Good. Go and do what I say. Bye.'

O'Keefe kissed his wife and put on his coat. 'I've got to go out.'

'You should take a hat,' she said, 'I think it's starting to drizzle.' She saw him to the door, calling the children down to be kissed. 'Bye!'

Elf took the tube to Camden Town, descending into the sweet, warm breath of the Northern line and fending off a man from the North Country who got in at the Angel.

'Ken, isn't it?'

'No.'

'Yes it is . . . Ken lad.'

'No it ain't Ken lad.'

'Oh . . . you a betting man?'

'Yeah. I bet you're going to get out of this carriage at King's Cross.'

The northerner chuckled. He wore a large grey suit to surround what would be (judging by his face) a large pink body, and he had a carefully mis-matched tie and breast pocket kerchief. He pulled the kerchief out and mopped at his brow as he chuckled.

'Very good. I've come down with a 'orse.'

'Couldn't afford the train then?'

'Good 'orse. 's in tomorrow. Interested?'

You've got to laugh. They must think we've just come up. Bleedin' northerners, watch too many fifties films. 'Like to buy some nylons?'

'No. Want to buy a watch?'

'What?'

'It's time you got out.' Kings Cross and the doors groan sluggishly apart, ''s your stop. I don't need your tip. I tell fortunes,' he leaned towards the fat little tipster, 'I can tell you that, as a prediction, if you don't get out here I'm going to clip your ear . . . got it?' Got it? The doors groaned again, shutting this time, and the guard shouted 'mind-the-doors' just after they closed. The northerner scurried up to the far end of the carriage and spent the trip to Euston ostentatiously avoiding Elf's glance.

At Camden Elf walked slowly up the High Street towards the canal. He stopped to phone Carol again.

'I'm sorry.'

'I'm not coming back again.'

'I know. I've just been so bloody useless. I'm sorry.'

'I'm happier now. We never loved each other.'

'Good. It's better that you're happier. Will you meet me for a drink?'

'No. There's no point, Elf. I'm looking for another job too.'

'You always are.'

'Yes. Have you been in touch with *your* family?'

'No, no point. Is Lance there?'

'No. He's still out. Didn't you get hold of him?'

'Yes. I did.'

He turned in the phone box and looked up towards the hump-back bridge over the canal. A dark figure in a long coat leaned on the wall there. He turned further and saw a car parking further up on the same side of the road as himself. Two very large black men climbed out. Number One was carrying a holdall. The car pulled away, leaving Little Maurice at the kerbside. He and Number One crossed. The figure in the long coat moved off the canal bridge, walking away from them.

'Elf! Elf!'

'I'm sorry. I shouldn't have rung. I've got to go now, Carol. I've got to.'

She rang off without trying to reply. Elf stood with the phone in his hand, watching the street. He turned. A change of traffic lights down the road and a burst of north-bound metal and rubber roared past, grown men vying to be first as if their car driving were the whole of life, for this moment. Elf turned again, at a door creak.

A woman, perhaps thirty-five or forty, trips unsteadily from the pub door which had creaked to allow her passage. She is joined soon (creak) by a rough-looking man in working-clothes and boots, and this man holds the woman's arm as they walk down the street. They argue, suddenly, and the man pushes his hand through his thinning hair in anguish, fingers apart and still holding on to her with his other arm, speaking loudly to her. They stop near Elf's phone box and the man draws the spread fingers slowly and painfully across his scalp and onto his face, then shouts something and spins the woman by her arm. The couple move on a little, away from Elf and arms closely entwined about each other, suddenly stopping under a street light and kissing fiercely. Soon the tension melts from their bodies and another tension takes over.

Elf could see the woman clearly, her blonde hair dyed so, it must be, and her tanny legs dyed also, but not the arms. She seemed a tawdry gift of womanhood and then Elf could see the man looking stunted and ugly and honest and he knew the woman was honest also, despite the dyeing.

A can clacked behind the phone-box as a cat crept past. Elf started, then smiled as he saw the cat. His eyes were accustomed enough to the dark that he could pick out a huddle of down-and-out in the doorway opposite, someone who'd missed his kip round the corner, or maybe didn't have the necessaries. A lorry growled and the lights down by Parkway changed again, releasing then nervously staunching a quick flow of traffic. Like a tourniquet. Elf avoided the headlamps to preserve the slight edge of night vision. It was no good, he'd looked into too many street lights and picked up enough of the headlamps. Something stirs in the shadows suddenly, but again it's the far side of the street and he can't make it out.

Elf replaced the handset to the phone, absently. He could see now. The dark figure in the long coat was passing again, and it had been his disturbed shadow that Elf had seen on the far side of the street. Under one of the lamps the man had dark, hollowed eyes and pale skin. He was joined by a half-caste, whore-looking woman. The two retreated into the shadows of Inverness Street, which had retired for the night as a market, but for the night only, so that there were scattered barrows at the kerbside and plenty of shadow there.

A white Transit van cruised past. Elf left the phone box and began to walk towards the canal bridge. A maroon car stopped beside him.

'Hey . . . Hicks.' O'Keefe climbed to stand next to Elf's shoulder and lay his hand upon Elf's forearm. 'What did I tell you to do?'

Elf didn't speak. Brian the Beard and another policeman Elf didn't recognize stood on the far side of the Hunter. The driver stayed behind the wheel. Brian smiled at Elf, but O'Keefe led Elf away from the kerb and back to the phone-box, trapping him by the glassed door and uneven paint.

'Go home, Hicks. I told you not to come. No one wants you here.'

Elf looked down at the side of the box. A stinking dark liquid escaped a plastic bag and came for his foot, trickling smoothly along the concrete. He shifted and looked at O'Keefe. There was some shouting from the direction of the lock, scuffle and shouting climbing uneasily and ungratefully from below the canal bridge. Elf made to speak, but O'Keefe held his hand up, palm flat.

A Ford Cortina drove past, fast, headlamps full on, lurching heavily on the uneven road surface. O'Keefe turned, calling to his driver. 'After them. Tell them to piss off.'

Brian the Beard climbed quickly in beside the driver and O'Keefe leaned, off balance and tripping forward as he shouted against the engine, 'Tell the bastards this one's ours. Tell them I say so and . . .' the car's tyres screamed as the driver let the clutch in, chasing the Cortina already stopped at the canal bridge and unloading its heavies. The white Transit van was on the bridge with its doors flung wide, seeming abandoned. O'Keefe turned, having regained his balance and finishing his sentence quietly, 'the Commander says so too.' He smiled at Elf and unconsciously pulled at his coat sleeves, adjusting. 'All this is beyond you, Alfred, so you should stick with my advice.'

A young, long haired man ran past them, then paused, pulling a pistol from his jacket as he turned, 'All right, Mr O'Keefe?'

'I'm all right, boy.' He released Elf's arm. 'Stop those two.' He pointed across the road to the sombre man in the long coat and the half-caste woman. They were running towards the bridge. O'Keefe turned to Elf again.

'Out of your league, Hicks. Stick with me. Do what I say. I'm a very clever man. I'll see you all right. You owe me two now. Don't forget. And do what I say. Go home, turn the telly on, forget this except that you owe me one more. Remember me when you're with your mates. If there's anything I want, give it to me. I'll look after you, that's how the likes of you and me work. Do what I say, and I say go home now.'

A thin film of drizzle had formed on O'Keefe's brown hair and he screwed his eyes up suddenly as if he were very tired. He patted Elf on the arm and trotted across to join the furious altercation that had developed where the young armed policeman had been despatched to stop the two Drugs Squad officers. There was much displaying of warrant cards and gnashing of teeth. The half-caste woman was almost throwing a fit, such was her anger. The long-haired subordinate of O'Keefe's was firm. O'Keefe was firm. Up on the bridge some more of O'Keefe's subordinates were being firm with the occupants of the Cortina. A second Transit came up with uniform police in it, and they took custody of the manacled Number One and Maurice, being very firm indeed.

Elf walked slowly towards the tube station. Above him, above the shops, people were poking their heads out of the windows of their flats to catch some of the action. To catch some of the drizzle. Another police car went past, sirens on. All they would catch was drizzle. Elf reached the tube.

'Ours, I believe.' O'Keefe smiled at the two Drugs Squad officers. The tall sombre man proffered his warrant card.

'Oh, I'm sorry. Ours, *sir*. Would you like transport, sir, or would you like to squeeze in with your companions down the road.'

'What's your name?'

'O'Keefe . . . D.I., sir.'

'You'll be sorry for this, O'Keefe.'

'I doubt it, sir. The Commander doesn't think so. I don't think he was very pleased to be considered untrustworthy. I don't think any of us are, *sir*.'

The tall man sighed but didn't answer. It had been a long haul and a lot of work and it was all cocked up, all because of the stupid girl he'd used. He'd have her filling out forms in Tilbury when he got hold of her . . . when he'd talked to her boss. He indicated to the half-caste girl that she should accompany him and walked past O'Keefe. The Detective Inspector smiled. He lit a cigarette and followed the tall man and the woman up towards the canal bridge, tugging at his shirt sleeves under the coat, to make sure the double cuffs were straight and the gold cufflinks would show just right when he got back to the nick. It would be a long night, he guessed. He'd phone the missus, tell her not to wait up and to kiss the kids for him. She wouldn't like it but there's only three years till he was out, and he was still young and they could go and live on the coast, which she would like and would be good for the kids. It was a rotten job but O'Keefe felt it was worth doing and believed he was an honest (all right, as honest as you'd get . . . still honest) man doing it to the best of his ability. He was probably right. He brushed the film of rain from his hair but let it stay on his face. He should have taken his wife's advice and brought a hat, but it looks so old fashioned. One of his D.C.s stood before him on the canal bridge.

'What have we got here, then, Ian?'

'A suspicious substance, sir, which I have impounded.' Ian smiled. O'Keefe smiled at the two Drugs Squad officers bending to confer with their colleagues in the Ford Cortina.

'Suspicious substance, sir . . . bit of luck, eh?'

The tall man stood upright and frowned at him. O'Keefe didn't mind, his governer would back him against these, and he wasn't looking for transfers or promotion.

Chapter Fifteen

Elf walked back from Old Street in the drizzle. It ceased as he reached the yard to the flats, as if by some design. The cars and rubbish were still in the yard and the lights in his flat were still on. The street lights wound their way towards him across the glistening tarmac, iridescent water snakes, forever changing, forever moving until they fade.

Claude had been around the flat with a vacuum cleaner and was now washing up.

'I should've married you.'

'I could think of reasons not to . . . what happened?'

Elf told him what he'd seen, the two men sitting side by side on the sofa and Claude silent all the time Elf was speaking.

'Will they cough, d'you think?'

Claude rubbed his hands, palms flat, up and down his face, then stood and walked to the far end of the room and leaned on the door.

'Not about anyone else. There's no reason for them to, since they'll be well looked after when they get out . . . even while they're in there. That Maurice will probably enjoy prison.'

'Why?'

'Butty man . . . but that's not the point. The fact is that Sir Lord John isn't going to be very pleased with us and your friend Boil won't be over the moon about his two thousand. 's better we go.'

'Where?'

'Bristol . . . Huddersfield, somewhere we're not known. Will the police be after us?'

'No. I'm not going anywhere, though.'

'Why?'

'I feel sick. I want to see things out. I'm not going anywhere.'

'I am. I'm going down the off licence for some whisky and in the morning I'm getting a bus somewhere,' Claude rocked forward off the wall, 'and that'll be that. Shall I bring the whisky back here?'

'If you want. Want some money?'

'No. I'm all right. What'll you do about that woman?'

Elf shook his head and turned the radio on. Claude left. There was some boring drone escaping the machine about how marvellous some new theatre was. He turned the dial. Some more boring drone from Fred of Hounslow who had called to explain how to solve the world's problems. Then George of Streatham had a go, then Daisy of Dudden Hill and Hilary of Hampstead. They all sounded the same, except Hilary who'd been hitting the cooking sherry and was cut off in her prime by the presenter.

Elf switched off. He picked up the phone and dialled Nancy's number. No answer. He thought to phone Lance and tell him what had happened but remembered how circumspect Nancy had been about the use of the telephone. He picked up one of a pile of paperbacks that lay on the coffee table, not caring which title or subject matter. *The Harder They Come* by Michael Thelwell. I don't think so somehow. He threw it at the clock, smiling at the ritual and missing. It was only a half hearted shot, Elf thought.

Upstairs the neighbours were playing rock music loudly. The music stopped and Elf could hear them arguing, knowing it was the daughter (rock music) and the father (church music and Glenn Miller). Glenn Miller came on, softly and politely, and he could hear the girl crying, also softly and now softer and now not at all. The music stopped. Elf could hear an argument in the street. He opened the window and leaned out, looking down the empty street towards the canal. A group of men were standing by the canal railings, he couldn't make them out clearly. Suddenly he saw a raised arm and a falling figure. Elf leapt back from the window, grabbed his keys from the table, and rushed out of the front door, slamming it. He took the stairs four at a time and was through the yard running to the canal in seconds. Only one figure was in the street, prone and unmoving by the canal railings. Elf slowed, trotting up to it. Claude. He lay with a complete stillness, a peaceful stillness, though the stillness could not, Elf knew, have been imparted by peaceful means. The whisky bottle was broken beside him and as Elf bent he could smell the alcohol on his friend's clothes. There was a large, broken gash on Claude's head. Elf tried to lift the head, but it was extremely heavy now and lifted awkwardly, so that he was frightened of hurting the man further. Elf could feel cold sweat on his own brow, now running into his eyes and across and down the bridge of his nose. Claude did not appear to be breathing. Elf knelt beside him.

'*Carol*!' and then quieter, 'Carol . . . call an ambulance, oh someone must be there . . .' and the last of these words drifted off into a whisper, so that he felt he'd said 'Claude needs an ambulance' but hadn't spoken the words at all. A voice behind him said,

'I shouldn't shout, Mr Hicks. It won't help him.'

And Elf's limbs were of lead and he believed he'd imagined the words so that he didn't turn but stayed kneeling. The voice said, 'Mr Hicks . . .'

Elf turned and stood to face Sir Lord John Bright. The small man wore a bulky three-quarter length leather coat, and without the sunglasses the eyes, Elf could see, even in this light, were puffy and tired looking. Bright smiled, almost, it seemed, an automatism with him. 'Your friend appears to have met with an accident. Hit and run, I would believe.' He smiled again, a parody of friendliness, like a bank manager; or a lawyer who knows you're going to get found guilty and is advising you to plead 'not guilty'. Or a landlord, that's it, thought Elf, a landlord as he takes your money.

'You bastard.' He moved forward, fists clenched.

'Oh I wouldn't do that.' Bright nodded behind Elf, who turned for a second, and saw the mini-toast and the bald, middle-aged enforcer. The bald man held a length of piping.

'I can still take you.' Elf was very frightened and very angry, cold angry.

'No.' Bright shook his head, 'you won't. It's finished. Go home. Your friend has had an accident. My friends have been unfortunate, I will lose their services for some time, and it will be very,' he paused for emphasis, '*very* expensive to me. It's over. You will have to deal with your party,' he swept his hand before him, open and palm up, holding its position at the end of the sweep, 'who will have taken a loss and I have taken a loss.

There are things I would like to ask you, but there is no time. Go home, Mr Hicks.'

'If I don't get you this time there'll be another. You'll have to keep an eye over your shoulder for me . . . d'you hear me?'

Sir Lord John Bright shook his head.

'In that case . . .' He closed the open hand into a fist and raised it to point with the extended index finger at Elf. 'We'll see to it now.'

Elf moved quickly to one side, hearing the swish of the piping by his ear. He held his leg out and tripped the rushing bald man, then turned to see the mini-toast drawing a long knife from his belt. Elf took two steps and took the canal railings in a gate-vault. He began to run down the tow-path, first a sprint to put some distance between them while the other men climbed the railings, then settling down into a fast but regular rhythm, knowing that he'd get pain soon and knowing that it would be better to take it in a regular stride than belt at it all the way and then have to slow. He stole a look over his shoulder. The mini-toast was running fast and steadily behind him. The bald man wasn't in it, already far behind and his short, powerfully thick legs unable to keep him going as fast as Elf and the mini-toast.

The pain came and then left and Elf turned it all on as the pain left, powering forward and regular breath, hump hump hump hump hump. He stopped to climb past some building equipment abandoned on the tow-path for the night. He looked again. The black boy was keeping up well, he must be a fit bastard. He'd lost the leather beanie. Elf ran on, Islington bound, his legs hot and sticking to the trousers, his shoes uncomfortable. They'd done about three-quarters of a mile now and he speeded up again, knowing that this was the time he could break the kid unless he were a runner, faster and faster. Elf looked again. Mini-toast was about sixty or seventy yards behind and was struggling, begining to wobble on his legs. Faster still for just a few seconds, Jesus that hurts but it'll hurt him more.

Elf stopped, feigning breathlessness, bending forward and moving close to the tow-path's edge. The mini-toast approached, knife in hand and whooping and screaming for breath, his face racked with pain, his lips drawn back. 'Gotcher, Hicks.' He held the knife tightly in his right hand and advanced. Elf stood upright, breathing fast but recovered now and moving closer still to the water. His legs were slightly apart and his arms loose by his sides. The black boy began his rush, holding the knife forward, 'Uuhuh,' and swinging the blade inwards as he came. Elf was much faster and simply stepped back, allowing the boy to fall through the space he had stood in and into the canal. He stayed down a long time and came up awkwardly.

'Help! Help!' The arms thrashed and the water foamed as he struggled under again and then screaming as he came up, 'Can't swim!'

'Hard luck son.' But Elf trotted along the path and took down the emergency lifebelt, throwing it to the boy. 'Here, someone'll fish you out in the morning.' He trotted away without looking to see whether the boy had made it to the lifebelt. Hard luck son. The night was cold. Bloody hard luck son. Elf trotted on, stretching his arms and breathing deeply, sometimes stopping to touch his toes and ensure the hamstrings didn't freeze up on him. He climbed the railings again and began to make his way back to the flats.

The tube to Wandsworth

Chapter Sixteen

Claude took a week to expire, victim to the effects of his 'accident' and lingering comatose in the London Hospital. Elf didn't visit. He had discovered his friend's whereabouts by telephoning Claude's home and speaking to his mother. He felt a heel for lying but he did it because he believed it was necessary. 'No, I didn't know, where is he? . . . and the police say it was hit and run? . . . oh, yes, that's near me but I haven't seen him for weeks. No . . . no, I don't think he could have been coming round, he usually phones first. He usually did . . . I'll try to get in to see him, missus. Should I take anything?' A long silence from Claude's mother while she gathered herself to say how it was with her son. 'No, don't take anything in, Alfred, he won't have any need for it. Nothing will help. They expected him to be finished when they turned the machine off but he's held on.' She sniffed and put her hand over the phone and Elf thought he could hear a little sob in the background and he thought, 'You bastard, Icks. You pure-born rotten bastard,' but he didn't know what else to do. Should he blurt it all out to the poor woman, that her son had caught it because he and Elfy had overstretched themselves getting involved with heavies and then I, Elfy, fucked it up and got your son caught out because of a bit of skirt? I done it, missus. It's down to me. I done it. I don't think it would help to tell you it wasn't an accident and that some bad bad black guys had tried to top him and then me. I had to leg it and when I come back there was an ambulance just leaving and a copper asking, 'Anyone see? Anyone know what happened?' and no one had seen so I crept past and kept me gob shut. Now it looks like they've managed to do him. It won't help you and it won't help me if I told you. It certainly won't bring him back.

Elf didn't visit. He saw no point in it and Claude's mother phoned back, sobbing clearly this time but unable to say what she'd called for so that Elf had said it for her and she'd agreed and rung off. And so that, Elf thought, was that. That was him. That was his and this is mine. Me.

Elf was puzzled by his own lack of involvement. He would have been able to justify this in terms of self-preservation but it simply wasn't true. He didn't want to be involved, this was his whole feeling. He didn't want to be involved with the demise of his friend, he didn't want to involve himself with the fate of Nancy though he knew he should do, he didn't try to contact Carol and he didn't try to find work. The most difficult move for Elf was to go towards some sort of appraisal of his own position, but the fact was he had no inclination to make any such appraisal.

Eventually, after several weeks, Elf had gone to Nancy's flat in Clapham. It was deserted, but the second time he visited, a week later, he'd found it occupied by a couple of young queens who'd taken it on a 'company let', which is merely a device for chiselling desperate people away from their rights. The queens had giggled a lot at him, peeking around their half-opened door but soon they saw he was no danger and offered a cup of tea. No, he didn't want any tea, thank you, but which agency did you get the let from?

They told him and he tried there, but it didn't help. Elf was greeted by a suave young man who wanted to know the nature of his interest and even as the suave young man said it Elf knew that nothing that he would say, no 'nature of his interest' would winkle the information out of this lot; and it was true. The young man was polite but firm, no, I'm sorry, sir, that's confidential, even *I* (as if he were some high priest of the property management business unlawfully excluded from the tabernacle), even *I* don't have any access to that sort of information about clients. If you would like to leave your name . . .

Elf left the name of a man that had taught him history when he was twelve and an invented address.

'Well sir, if by any chance we hear from her I'll make sure your details are passed on,' and he smiled Elf to the door, 'if that's all then, Mr Minto, I'll say goodbye.' Sweaty handshake. As he walked down the street Elf could see the man go to the telephone at the back of the shop-type estate agent's office and the dolly-bird typist came to the plate glass door to stare after him.

During the weeks that followed, the beginning of winter, Elf descended into a state of torpor. He stopped the daily running. He stopped *any* running. He had no regular social contacts. He had no wish for any, and he certainly had no wish for regular contact with Lance, even by telephone. Elf was glad when it finished.

Lance had originally phoned four or five times a day to enquire about his money, but he eased off soon (he had no choice, since Elf didn't have the money) and Elf suspected there may have been some intercession on his behalf by Carol. Or perhaps there was some intrusion on the part of Lance's honour code, so that it would be (and Elf could imagine him saying it) 'really bad news' to go around throttling his brother-in-law or having his arms broken by a subby, even ever-such-a-little-bit broken.

Carol had moved out of Lance's place and found a bedsit, Elf knew, but he didn't have the energy to try to contact her except through the Boil. Perhaps even then to turn Elf over, an action fully in character for Lance, would have been 'really bad news'. Whatever the reason he didn't give Elf as hard a time about the money as Elf had expected. Then he called one day and suggested splitting what he referred to as 'our business loss'. Elf agreed to that but didn't see where he'd get the money and said so. Lance didn't call any more after that day because the phone had been cut off. During the last call Lance had gone on to one of his favourite theories, about it being a business expense, and 'you've got to speculate to accumulate, son, that's one of the lessons I've learnt in this here life, know what I mean?' Elfy had said yes and could imagine Lance tugging at the collar of his silk shirt as he explained away the loss (more for his own benefit, of course, than Elf's). There was a 'put any spare dough to work, know what I mean, no good tying it up down the bank' speech which came as a sort of matched set with the 'speculate to accumulate' one and Elf had heard them both many times and knew it was to follow soon so he claimed there was someone on the doorstep, I'll have to go, yeah, I'll have to go. Ta-a, cock . . . yeah, ta-a. On reflection Elf thought he may have witnessed the genesis of one of Boil's anecdotes: 'topped out . . . yeah, large

153

scotch in there, mate . . . two grand, I done on it, know what I mean? Last time I get involved with wogs, I can tell you. Unreliable. *Two grand.*' And this would be delivered at some saloon bar table and would be meant to impress upon the listener, 'I am such a rich and boastful bastard I can take a two grand caning and not go boracic . . . didn't I tell you before what a bleedin' tastee-freeze I was?'

Elf knew then, as he considered, what it must feel like to have known the Boil since the beginning, as an early cell mate in Ashford or somewhere when he was a kid. Elf had plenty of time to consider things now, and he sat and looked at the phone, considering, before saying out loud:

'Course you're a tough guy, Boil.'

He looked away from the telephone and thought out loud, 'I'm going barmy sitting here'; but he said nothing.

Elf had plenty of time to think about following up his threat to Sir Lord John Bright, since the card from British Telecom came the next day, 'we are about to cut off your telephone' and neither Boil nor anyone else could disturb his solitude. There was no follow-up on Elf's part and, more surprisingly, there was no follow-up from Bright. Elf was sure that the attack on him would be pursued further, but it never was. After a few days of the quickened pulse and dry mouth every time he saw black guys hanging around the flats looking as if they'd nothing in particular to do, Elf came to the conclusion that if anything were to happen then there was no real way to dodge it and he would be better served to take it as it comes, take it easy. He couldn't take it easy but he took it eas*ier* and stopped slinking in and out of his own front door. Besides, being tense about that would not have fitted very comfortably with the inertia which was the rest of his life.

And in this way Elf came to the winter. The days became an endlessly repeated symmetry layed one on one on one, end to end and endless with a regular (every second Tuesday, Box 4 over there and bring this card . . . do you want a B.1? And the giro turns up every second Saturday with fifteen minutes to spare before the Post Office shuts) interruption which isn't enough to disrupt the feeling of endlessness but instead is a kind of contrapuntal reinforcement of the theme.

One mid-November week (Elf wasn't sure which except it was a non-signing week at Box 4 over there) he was stopped by

O'Keefe in the street, a car sidling up to him and O'Keefe alone in it.'

'Get in, Alfred. Let's go for a ride.'

After a brief interrogation, 'who you running around with now?' style, O'Keefe came to the real reason for the visit. Elf was asked to pick up a package from this place and deliver it to that. He did so the same day and was rewarded with £5 and his cab fare for his trouble.

'Don't forget, Hicks, see anything I want, bell me. I'll make sure you don't lose out on nothing.'

You must think I'm the Krays and Richardsons all rolled into one, Mr O'Keefe.

'Yes, Mr O'Keefe.'

Bollocks, Mr O'Keefe. Did you know I was moving to Vladivostok next week? No? Well I am, no doubt. I'll drop you a card when I get there. No doubt you could call me up, 'See anything I want, Alfred, bell me. Any naughty little reds misbehaving, know what I mean, long arm of the law and all that.' 'Yeah, course mate. I'll tell you what, there's a vodka drinking ring here, thousands of them in it. Wicked, it is. I'll tell you where you can cop them.'

Sometimes Elf walked the streets, then often Elf walked the streets, no jobs available so he wasn't looking for one, not looking for anything in particular nor going anywhere in particular; just filling in time before he dies, like the rest of the world, just slam the door and get out of that stinking flat, with his coat buttoned tight against the winter's freezing wind, the snow queen farts, and having farted moves on. Always walking walking walking; Old Street, Clerkenwell Road or possibly a wander round Burnhill Fields, sometimes take the Clerkenwell route and down Theobald's Row or even dropping south through Hatton Garden and passing the lunchtime madness of rushing office girls at Leather Lane and the two pints and a cheese sandwich, kipper tie and quilted jacket (so they look like the Michelin Man) office boys, outside Henekey's going in or inside Henekey's coming out. Maybe. Elf never went in the place. Opposite he could stop and look at the travel agent's notices and other signs in the sports shops, 'Book early for the best ski resorts.' 's right mate, well in the last resort, which it'll be when I can afford it, I can always go and chat up me bank manager, talk to the mutt-and-jeff bank.

Elf turned away from the window and continued westwards along High Holborn. The wind carried light drops of rain, didn't it? Wasn't that one? Then two and another and another. Yes, now definitely many and he could see it on the ground, a rash of darker spots on the paving stones and then his hair was stuck wet to his forehead and still he walked on, into Chancery Lane, through an alley, into Lincoln's Inn, which has got a church which appears to be for members only (*there's* an idea) and is very firmly for members only when it's pissing down outside, the lawyers don't want no hoi-polloi polluting their solace with their smelly raincoats and half-eaten sandwiches. There's a lawn you can use by kind permission of the master and you begin to wonder who the hell are these men that they seem to have annexed our heritage, *why* can't you look? Now he turned into Lincoln's Inn Fields which is all deserted tennis courts during the winter and a shuttered tea hut, steel tables grouped together outside for warmth and for the comfort, each insensitive plasticised skin, of the other. Confused looking tables that clutch the tea-stain memory of an old summer.

Elf moved on to Cuvent Garden, which is how anyone who's *anyone* says it, cuvent, then north again and east into Charing Cross Road where you could buy a drum kit or an electric piano to form a band with, a street you could get your music published in, become famous and rich in and then impotent and rich (though these don't follow each other – necessarily) and then it's a street you can join the rest of the tossers in, watching 'what the butler would have seen if only he'd remembered his bleedin' binns' or buy ever more exotic electrically driven objects to fill spaces that the poor man struggling under the weight and pressure of his own success (sold the drum kit and bought a recording studio) couldn't fill unaided, American Express, that'll do nicely sir, there's your apparatus then. The success story could take it home to his cuddles, 'Hey up, darling, look what I've got. Better than a flaccid old plonker, eh?'

You can buy all this in Charing Cross Road, and literature too from a house of high literature than would flay and pickle trade unionists given the chance or invoke the Combination Laws (they may well soon get a chance). You could teach yourself Latvian or Estonian further up, or further still Spanish dancing lessons (*real* ones) and you could turn left thankfully to get out of it, as Elf did, and it was still raining buckets. Sutton

Row gives surprisingly onto Soho Square with thick grass on it and a tree or two that are as surprised as you are that they're there. It's still busy with plenty of cars but it's so *upright*, that Soho Square, compared with its name and its surroundings, all film companies and finance companies and posh estate agents, and suddenly it's Dean Street, where, should Elf have been one of the poor, struggling, successful rich men with his newly acquired apparatus in his packet (batteries extra) and a distinct lack of turgidity in his tonker (did I say plonker before?), he could press the top bell and rent himself some Spanish lessons (the other ones) or French lessons or Swedish lessons owing to the cuddles in Carshalton being morally opposed to KY let alone any of his little stunts, electrically driven or otherwise. She (Carshalton) is right to oppose it if she doesn't like it but not because she's morally finer, oh no, it's just that if our boy wonder (he must have stopped next to you at the traffic lights with his electric sunroof and all that crap) didn't behave like a bull in a china shop she wouldn't need no KY. God it's cold here . . .

. . . cold cold cold cold, bloody wind freezing ice-your-brain-up cold here, and the rain rains like someone's stuck a funnel down the collar, so goddamn cold and a nasty shiver would run up your back so that if you didn't get inside and dry soon it wouldn't be any good for you but it depends whether you've enough spirit left in you to care, enough care to spirit, enough money for pub spirit. Grey slab buildings shuffle past and Elf doesn't have enough spirit left to care but just gets and stays wet. All the grey slabs are shoulder to shoulder and streaks of rain and grime slime stain hang below the window ledges like the ghosts of window boxes but you need light to grow flowers and there's no light here, no flowers, blumen hell, so to speak, just dust joined with the rain that should have been channelled away by the broken guttering above and isn't so it pours a steady sheet from the roof to the window ledges and the lichen gets its chance.

Suddenly (again suddenly) Elf found himself in Oxford Street, soaked to the skin and opposite the black-marbled pillars of the emporium which employed his wife. Elf stood there watching the doors and tried to imagine her measuring window netting, 'one metre, no sir, I don't think you're getting it right. That's the *drop*. For a window like that you'd need, oh, let's see . . .' He knew she hated it. The imagining wasn't going very well and he found it hard to visualize her features individually. Why was that? Elf leaned on the wall opposite the emporium and pondered, first on his wife's face and then why he couldn't even do that. He felt weak and his breath came slowly and stiffly to him, tight chested breath. His forehead cold sweat was perhaps perspiration or perhaps rain, he couldn't tell.

Elf tried to move forward. He found it hard to judge the speeds and distances of the buses and taxis and heavily laden tourists struggling by with their shopping booty.

'Sorry missus, sorry,' but she didn't speak English or didn't appear to and shouted at Elf in some foreign tongue which was muffled by his inability to concentrate on it. Elf swept away from her, hands thrust deep into the pockets of his sodden coat. He managed to cross Oxford Street and stood before the emporium for a second before he shouldered his way through the crowds sheltering under its eaves.

Elf leaned on the wall. Gold letters were cut into the black marble, allowing that this man had ordered the building built (what a philanthropist!) and that that man had ordered it done in such a way and not any other and that another had opened it. He squeezed his eyes. He squeezed his brain to concentrate, oh . . . the Hon. Mrs . . . sorry, that *woman* had opened it.

The rain had made Elf's coat stink and he was very conscious of it, so that he would have stood away from people if he could. He could feel the cold water running onto his shirt, tight-buttoned coat or no tight-buttoned coat. He put his hand inside the coat and was surprised to find that *all* his clothes were soaked and freezing. Elf's body felt strangely warm. His chest became tighter still and his head became thick; cheeks, nose and lips cold, almost numbed. There was a pain in the lower part of Elf's gut and he felt that he should find somewhere to rest soon or he'd topple over. He leaned against the black marble facing and closed his eyes, fingering the lettering absently, feeling the gold colour. His blood was as water flowing through his body, no strength and no power to be gained from the flow. He should eat, he knew, but he wasn't hungry. Food would increase the stomach pains (at first anyway) or he might vomit all over Carol's employer's nice black marble.

I could go in and see her, he thought, quickly realizing that it was impossible. He saw his reflection in his mind's mirror window, and knew he'd look like a down-and-out. *Spare's tanner for a cuppa tea, guv?* She would throw a fit.

Elf opened his eyes and looked up, seeing through the crowd a brown head and bobbing black hair running past in the gutter. Elf pushed desperately to the kerbside, perhaps it's Claude. A tall black man leapt on the bus he'd been chasing and turned, smiling from the shelter of the bus platform, displaying a high brow and tribal marks, three on each cheek, to wave happily through the rain to some companion left on the pavement.

Elf left the kerb, moving unsteadily across Oxford Street again, ignoring the traffic, neither knowing of nor caring for the wind and rain now. He plunged into Bond Street Tube station, buying a ticket, any ticket, fifty pence, 'ere are then mate, just give us a ticket. He staggered down to the platform. The pain that had been at the base of his gut was joined now by another pain, running from the top of the skull down across his left eye and freezing the nose and cheek muscles much more successfully than any wind or rain would have managed, and the pain for the eye and the pain for the head and the pain for the gut bottom set off by someone piling weight upon weight on his chest. The left eye, the source he knew now of all pain, wasn't focussing properly. There's nowhere to get glucose on a tube station . . . there is! The chocolate machine. He wandered the length of the station, stumbling until he pushed past some skinheads and found a machine. It was broken. Elf shook the tray but it stayed broken.

He moved away again, aware that people were staring. Elf leaned back on the tiles and closed his eyes. A rumble from the far tunnel and a breath of air as a train entered. He opened his eyes and looked up. Two youngsters, kids of about ten or eleven were amusing themselves by looking at him. One grew serious and said, 'You all right, mister?'

He nodded. Past the children a man approached the chocolate machine. He was bending forward to peer at the trays and was wearing a three-quarter length leather coat. He was a short man and wore no hat. He pulled himself upright from inspecting the broken machine (maybe it contained some of *his* money), Elf could see a pair of sunglasses. Bright.

Elf pushed through the skinheads again. He dug Bright

sharply in the back with his fist, and spitting the word, 'Bright.'

As the man turned Elf punched. A hard punch, as hard as he could to the body, one two. He didn't want or need to talk, only needing the punch. The man threw up his arm to defend himself and Elf kicked at the shins. A cheer went up from the skinheads.

'Oi! Oi! Ruck dahn 'ere! Ruck!'

They gathered around. Elf punched at the body more, three four five six. He lost count, only careful not to punch at the head, he didn't want to put his subject out and finish it. The man hadn't spoken or protested. He hadn't, strangely, lost his sunglasses either. Elf had lost all pain and tiredness now. He took the man by the coat and dragged him to the wall, throwing the light body against the wall, once, twice.

'Oi! . . . Oi!' The cheer went up again and Elf was aware of being closely surrounded by cropped hair and big grins, 'Go on me son, oi! oi! oi!'

A brave London Transport station hand tried to force his way through, but the skins stopped him.

'Oi! Oi! Fuckin' ruck the black bastard, go on, give 'im some of that!'

Elf wasn't hearing them. Sometimes he saw flashes of their faces as he turned and hit, turned and hit. He threw the man again against the wall. The man landed on the chromed metal of the chocolate machine. A woman shrieked and Elf possessed himself enough to hear it and to wonder why the bald man or the beanie hadn't been there to stop him. The man's body hit the wall slowly and his head hit the machine slowly. The woman's scream came slowly. Baldy and the beanie were being as slow as all hell today. Where are they? Elf's victim's back arched and he fell motionless at Elf's feet, leaving a clear smear of blood on the metal '2x10p' sign and the reject button. The sunglasses had come off now at last and the man's head, smashed, and the glasses, smashed, lay beside each other. Elf bent forward, looking at the white bone showing through the scalp. He felt sick. The skinheads were chanting and jeering.

A train roared in but the guard didn't open the doors. His carriage came to rest in front of Elf and his victim. The guard stood fixed in his open doorway, looking at the scene on the platform for a few seconds. The skinheads jeered. Elf stood still. The guard stayed still, watching. The would-be passengers stood still on the platform, patiently waiting. Elf's victim lay still, bleeding being his only movement. The passengers squeezed up against the windows to see what was going on. Someone in the guard's carriage shouted at him. He turned his back and spoke to the driver over the intercom warning.

What the guard saw, instead of the Bond Street shopping-and-office crowd he usually expected, was a mob of jubilant hooligans shouting and skipping, then a big open space, twenty or thirty feet long open platform, in which stood a white-faced, crumpled-damp-coated young man and at his feet the prone figure of a West Indian. The guard knew a racist attack when he saw one. At the end of the big space that had been allowed for the fight were the usual afternoon passengers, some watching the scene before them, others desperately trying to believe it wasn't there, not hadn't happened, just wasn't there.

The guard saw the blood on the platform and he looked up and saw blood on the wall, smeared and splashed. There was a drying red streak on the tiles. He thought it looked like an abbatoir as much as anything. The guard looked at the tiles and thought of his wife and son and was apprehensive. As he thought about it he knew he was frightened, not 'apprehensive' but he also knew what would be his duty to do. This isn't any part of the duty of a London Transport guard but is what some men see as their duty when presented with a problem, as some men (and women) pick up drunks in the street and dust them off, 'where you going, then?' He spoke into the intercom again and swallowed hard, stepping forward and, trying to indicate to the passengers in his carriage 'stay there' with a low sweep of his hand, he stepped through the doorway. The moon faces crowded closer to the glass, green lit. Some came and peered around the guard's open doorway.

The train guard bent forward and turned over the figure on the floor. He got blood on his hands turning the man and he supressed an urge to vomit. It has to be done. The platform was silent save for the scuff of shoes from people descending the last of the steps and joining the crowd, 'What's happened?' 'Oh, it's down there, you can't see properly.' The eyes of the man the guard had turned were open and unseeing. There was no puffiness. The man wasn't visibly breathing.

The guard stood upright and looked into the face of the crumple coated man standing before him. Elf. This man had blood on his hands, from his own, self-inflicted cuts and from the West Indian. There was a long dark stain down the front of his old coat. He looked to the guard as if he needed a wash. He was unshaven. His eyes were glazed and he was unsteady on his feet. All these things registered for ever in the guard's mind. He moved gently and carefully forward. Everyone on the platform who could see and all those in the tube train windows were straining to stare at the guard and Elf. Some admired the guard. Some wished he'd get on with it. Some wished they'd got another train, why the hell'd I get on this one, jesus she'll never keep waiting this time. Or my dinner will be cold. Or the wife will have trouble parking the Ford Escort at Gant's Hill for this long. Or no one'll be there to pick the kids up from school, oh I knew it wasn't worth leaving work early. One woman sat, uselessly and stupidly, unable to think how she might break the news of her vocation to her parents. She fumbled a rosary in her pocket, it's always a good time to start up a novena, living is praying, hail mary, I wonder what's going on down there, hail mary I hope our dad doesn't get fighting angry, hail mary I want to go home and prepare for it, living is praying, hail mary the continuous communion, hail mary I hope the train hasn't broken down, hail mary can't you please please intercede and let me get on with drinking from my bitter cup, hail mary I don't want to look at the join at the vee in that young man's jumper, oh he's so lovely warm looking, how many's that now . . . oh it doesn't matter. Our father, who art in heaven, bitter aloes be thy main (consumption . . .) Oh lord, I've got it all mixed but that curly hair in the vee looks so warm.

If the guard had had the strength of the woman's convictions he would have called upon them. All he had was his own courage and that seemed precious little to him. All the same he spoke softly and quietly to the man who'd made the racist attack, ever conscious of his own light brown skin. He moved forward slowly and gingerly took hold of Elf's arm, as if it were a stick of dynamite.

'You'd better come and sit down mate. You look all done in.'

Elf nodded, yes I should. He was very tired. He tried to step forward but his legs wouldn't have it, and the train guard carried him over to the carriage, holding the thin body awkwardly in one arm as he reached up for the door release to free his passengers.

Chapter Seventeen

The area was cosy and the street was cosy, suburban curved repetition cosiness street. No bus route, no yellow line. Tidy. There were new cars parked along the curved kerb, neatly parked and punctuated here and there by an old banger, perhaps the property of some artisan who'd scraped together the necessaries, taking his betters at their word, and he'd rushed down with his hard earned treasure that neither moths nor rust will devour to claim his semi. The artisan couldn't live up to his house yet, so the neighbours would have to put up with the banger outside, consoling themselves only that he'd be promoted one day and graduate to a new motor.

Two or three of the houses had heavily verdant, unclipped hedges, hedges that dipped with their own weight and the winter rain, hedges looked upon by unwashed windows. Should you peer around the hedge you might see an abandoned roller-skate chassis, bootless and rusting in an unkempt garden, yellow grass marking some recently moved door or buckled hardboard. Four dustbins, A,B,C,D, and only the latter two having lids. Bed-sits. Some pity-the-poor-immigrant would come every fourth Friday to take possession of his rent, or the rent of the man for whom he was an agent. We imported these, when we were importing, along with the decent-man-immigrant; and the rentier-immigrant attending every fourth Friday is considered among the most successful immigrants by English liberal standards, only behind the academics and shopkeepers as the best integrated of all, not like the noisy junglies in Brixton or Stoke Newington, rioting and causing trouble all over the place. Up the landlords. Right up.

In her austere little room on the first floor Carol was blow drying her hair. She told herself that she was happier here than as a half welcome guest with Lance and Noleen. In many ways she *was* happier. She had independence. If it wasn't for the long tube journey to work . . . if it wasn't for the damp room, so small and ugly . . . if it wasn't for the soupy yellow light in the morning and there's God knows how long to spring, my whole life . . . if it wasn't for all this (here she swung with the hair dryer, indicating the room to herself). Carol brought the hair dryer to her head again and swung her hair in the warm air, enjoying it.

The room Carol had indicated to herself was coated in an extraordinary collection of dark paint, sombre browns, greens and a blue skirting board competing with a ceiling painted 'raven'. She was assured by the landlord that 'raven' had been specially chosen for the last tenant, and at great expense. Like the scratchy wardrobe and the rickety chest of drawers and the single bed always smelling of mildew, eh? The last tenant must have had very peculiar tastes. Still, it's my own room.

The window was stuck with brown paint, layer on layer all on top of layers of some other hideous colour, all firmly stuck to the frame so that she couldn't open it to air her room; but it was her space. Carol smiled gently and brushed gently, playing the dryer's warm air over the back of her head and shoulders. The light went out and the dryer stopped. Alone in the darkness without the sound of the dryer Carol was suddenly aware of the rain at her window. She listened for a second, then fumbled under the bed for her handbag and tip-toed across the lino floor for the meter. Click. She turned the handle on her fifty pence. The light and the blower came on. Carol clicked the handle on another fifty pence.

The hair-dryer was blowing across the bed, and the air flow fluttered her nylons hung on the back of the one chair. Carol picked the dryer off the bed and ran the warm air over her head, then her face and breasts. She was pleased by the innocent pleasure of her own sensuality. The doorbell rang. That's my one. That's my bell. Carol held her hair-towel across her breasts, tucking it under the armpits and holding her elbows awkwardly close to herself to support it. Since she left Elf she had permed her hair, so that it fell now in damp, sweet-smelling ringlets about her ears and cheeks. Carol liked this sensation and gave herself time for it, even though she was being rushed by the doorbell ring again.

She pulled the curtain aside and lifted the net, peering through the rain-beaded glass. A car waited outside the door, its lights shining on an old Marina belonging to the man in the next room. A big shiny car. The doorbell ringer stepped back to the pavement and waved up at her, holding his black umbrella high to do so.

'Carol!' His call drifted, muffled and quieted, through the glass.

Carol waved back, awkwardly because of the towel, and dropped the curtain back into place as he turned, presumably to put the car's light out. She put on a dressing gown and slippers and began the descent to the door.

'Charles . . . hi.' She stood behind the door, pulling the gown closer about herself.

'Hullo.' Charles was a tall man in his early twenties, whose hair had prematurely greyed, making him seem older. He'd left the umbrella in the car this time, and there were dewy drops of water gathered on his brow. 'Can I come in?'

'Yes. Of course.'

Carol smiled for him and held the door back to let him in. The young man smiled back; he smiled too much, she thought, and looked unlucky. So what? Carol had decided she wasn't going to care too much for luck. Good luck only meant bad luck sometime, she knew that, but a good long shot of bad luck never meant you were entitled to good luck in the future, like a pension, or an investment plan. Elf looked like he should be lucky and he never really was. *We* never were and look what happened to us, Carol. For now I'd better not think about lost chances with a man I loved once. For now I'd better concentrate on being here and staying as happy as I've made it. For-now-Charles has a good job in insurance and a Granada to go with it. For-now-Charles was always polite and took her out for meals and cinemas, always wearing a tie and jacket and his hair clipped close to his boring empty head. Charles didn't try to make passes all the time but did enough to let her know he knew which end to use. Carol thought she liked him. He was very correct and smiled a mock embarrassment for her dressing gown.

For now he would do, Carol thought, better than the last creep with his unwashed socks and electric guitar, 'I fought I could kip dahn 'ere, eh?' . . . well *he* thought. For now Charles was miles better than that, she thought as she smiled polite smile back into his polite smile mask, and Carol thought this with no unkindness nor bitterness for the man. He was a benchmark after Elf. A kindly, worthy benchmark. Carol leaned forward and kissed him on his Chanel cheek, and for-now-Charles leaned to accept the kiss.

'I'm sorry. I didn't realize the time. My hair's wet. Want a whisky while you wait?'

'Yes. If it's okay. We've an hour before our table's due.'

'You booked a table?' She was pleased, though she would've been surprised if he hadn't.

'Yes.'

In her one room Carol set the young man on the one chair and gave him whisky and water.

'Flat tap water, I'm afraid.'

'I prefer the round.' The smile again and her polite return. Charles perched on the edge of his chair, gently rocking his whisky glass and watching as she lowered herself onto the edge of the bed and began blowing again at her hair.

'Pass me the brush.'

He did, but fumbled, dropping it at Carol's feet, and they both leaned to pick it up, bumping heads and laughing. They kissed. Suddenly his hand was inside Carol's dressing-gown, palm cupping the breast.

'I'm sorry. I'm sorry . . . come here, Carol.'

'Don't be sorry.' She switched off the blower and knelt forward to kiss him again in comfort, and then they laughed again in the kiss.

'Don't be sorry,' again, as the whisky glass falls also to the ground, dampening the linoleum in a swiftly spreading puddle, but small.

They move back onto the pink candlewick and struggle with his tie and already Carol's thinking of Elf, go away Hicks, go away. Her stiff and correct young man, correct for a mortage (Hicks), correct for already owning a Granada in his young years, stiff for the moment, kisses her correctly, his hands smelling of the spilled whisky as he pushes the gown back over her shoulders, as he pushes back her other life, beatha-Elf spilt. Only I can do that, truthfully, she thinks. Now her energy is released, pulling at his belt and poppop popping the shirt buttons. They laugh again, kissing still, and soon are one and even sooner Carol lies prone by the unopened door of a quiet and ivy clad garden, rich velvet green grass behind a tall wall and she was become the woman who had been another, with another, and had been another Carol's Carol, belonging in grief to a memory (but having no grief, him or her). Elf was now outside the wall, how can some act mean so much? Carol didn't know, but it was true for her, and she felt grieved. Would Elf ever be grieved by this? She squeezed the man beside her and thought not. She turned to look at the dozing man. His face, broad nose, wide lips and chin running to fat, even at his young age. Perhaps he had always run to fat. 'Never *not* run to fat,' Carol said to herself, touching his brow, 'and I've been missing that . . . but, but. I wish some of you was him, even though that's the most evil thought I could have now, and so unfair to you . . .

'It's cold and damp now in this ivy clad garden and I want to leave now. I don't want to think like this.'

'We should get up. We'll miss our table.' Charles' eyes were open and were looking at her. How long has he been looking? How much does he know? Carol sat up quickly, pulling the gown over her shoulders.

'Turn round and I'll put my dress on.'

'I love you, Carol.' He had his back to her and was buttoning his shirt.

'Don't be silly . . . oh I'm sorry, I don't mean that,' she turned and touched him, 'but you hardly know me. You shouldn't just say it.'

'I'm not. I mean it. I love you. When you get divorced I'll ask you to marry me.' He turned, suddenly and stood. Carol could see his young paunch being folded away with the shirt-tails. 'I will ask. I'm asking now.'

'Let's go and have dinner, Charles. Let's go now. I'll put my shoes on.'

'I *am* asking. I've got money saved and a good job and I'll get promoted soon. "I love you," I said. You don't have to say you love me yet.'

He stood there with his half-buttoned trousers anxious young face. I'm not going to get younger, Carol thought, not from now on.

'I mean it, Carol. You don't have to be with someone for ages to fall in love and I'm not asking you to rush straight into anything. Just agree things between us ... quietly ... you know.'

He should have touched her then, but his inexperience didn't allow it. Carol nodded. She knew what he meant. She had wanted, all through her short marriage to Elf, the sort of secure and serious life this secure and serious young man offered.

'You don't have to ask me to marry just because we've made love once, Charles.'

Carol turned her back to him. The young man had his jacket on again now and brushed its arms gently with his hand and he came around to face her again and speak.

'I know. I'm not a fool. I know I look boring, but I want it to be good for us ... I know.'

Carol swept her new-permed hair before her face with her flat hand, holding it there and weeping quietly and softly into it.

'Come on. We'll be late.' Charles pulled her hand away as he spoke, and touched her shoulder gently through the hair.

'You don't have to say you love me just because we've screwed once. I don't expect it.' She sobbed lightly now.

'I don't believe you've said that.'

'Well I did. I'm sorry. I'm not sure about things.'

'It's okay. People get depressed. I would, in this dump.' Charles' arms were around Carol's shoulders and his embrace was firm. 'Sort the divorce out, Carol, and we'll get you out of this.'

Carol nodded and stopped crying soon, though she hadn't stopped feeling rotten. Charles held her coat up for her. As they left the front door in the coinbox in the hallway rang, but they ignored it, concentrating instead on running through the rain to Charles' car. The rain had fallen heavily throughout the day and was still falling, so that deep cold puddles snatched and spat at Carol's ankles as she ran.

The engine burst into life and so did the stereo, lights cutting through the streaming rain and the wipers push a sheet of water from the screen. Two faces laugh, happy and expectant for their evening, as the car moves off, street light thrown through the screen illuminating the woman running her fingers through her curled hair to release the rainwater gathered during the run to the car. When they stop at the 'T' junction she leans over and kisses his cheek, and they are both comforted in their steel shell against the rain.

The coinbox phone in the hallway to Carol's bedsit rings on and on. Eventually a mousey girl steps sleepily from her ground floor room and answers.

'Hicks? I don't know any Mrs Hicks . . . oh, *Carol*. No. She's out. No, I don't know where . . . ring who? Police? Okay. I'll get a pencil. Hold on.'

Chapter Eighteen

On his third visit to Michael Cummings, Elf was able to see the room properly. He was surprised to find that he'd made his previous visits to this place in some sort of daze. He hadn't felt dazed at the time; but the fact is that, though it was a mere five days since he'd been in the room, Elf felt as if he'd never been there.

Michael Cummings looked as Elf believed he should look, blue-eyes tinging grey, early, worried creases to his skin, and a surprising 'outdoor' look to him, red-brown tan still as if he'd just been in Florida or . . . maybe he had. There's no reason why not. Elf eased himself into the chair as Cummings' hand indicated, careful of that bruise . . . ah! He looked to Cummings but the man was pre-occupied. Elf looked around. The room was small, much smaller than he'd believed, and was definitely the man's office rather than an interview room. There was a bookcase along one wall with a row of yellow text books on one of its shelves. There was a parquet floor, so frequently polished over the years that the edges of the wooden slats were proud where they met and blackened with the drag of varnish and polish over the prominence. The walls were drab grey, interrupted only by the small bookcase and a window overlooking the western corner of the South Block.

Beyond the South Block Elf could imagine the green common that should be. He'd been on the common several times as a kid, and now that it was tantalizingly close but unavailable to him he grew nostalgic for the Wandsworth Common of his youth, and wished that he'd paid it closer attention when he'd been free to roam it at will. He wished he'd been sitting in a different part of the prison van coming in, so he could have seen on the way, that would have helped. Elf imagined the common as best he could while he waited for Cummings; the scampering dogs and responsible looking women in thick tweed skirts strolling from their Victorian houses. Cars parked with canoodling lunch-time lovers, rain upon the polished paintwork of the car and condensation and guilty looks within. If Elf turned so he could look across towards Trinity Road there was bound to be at least one retired man with a 'military bearing', striding. Elf turned again and looked at the outside of the prison wall. He preferred it out here, and the walls were better looking.

'What happened to your eye, Hicks?'

'Everyone asks that, sir. I fell over.'

Elf stared at the man. He'd asked the question but he didn't appear to be interested in the answer. Perhaps if I tell him I had a bundle with the pervert they've stuck me in a cell with it'll perk him up. Then he'll know all I'm good for. Fighting. Michael Cummings was flipping back through his notebook and slowly shaking his head just a very little, so that the movement would be imperceptible to any but the most attentive watcher. Cummings wasn't interested in Elf for today. Today he was just going through the movements, for the sake of form, not merely for the prison service, but for the sake of form for himself, so that he should remain occupied. He was totally absorbed by the letter his wife had left that morning, a 'Dear John', or, in his case, 'Dear Michael', and he knew that concentrating on Hicks' (or on anyone's) problems would save him having to think about himself and his beloved. Ex-beloved, now presumably ensconced in a b & b in Bath or Brighton with her eighteen-year-old lover. He allowed his head to shake slowly from side to side again as he tried to find the place where he'd left off with Hicks last. He should have done it before the prisoner arrived, Michael knew, but he hadn't and had become instead re-absorbed in himself so that the warder's polite knock had been a shock.

'I don't want to be here today, sir. I don't s'pose it's possible . . .'

Cummings began looking through some papers on his desk, suddenly and very actively, shuffling the leaves and spreading them until he found what he wanted. He allowed Elf to wait a little longer while he read the sheet of paper, then jammed it back into the paper tray, gathering the spread papers from his desk and shoving them on top. Cummings picked up the biro and pad. Act over, thought Elf.

'Now. We'd talked about your friends, hadn't we? I'd like today to look at your marriage.' *Your* marriage. There was a keenness in Michael Cummings' tone and a shine in his eyes which Elf mistakenly believed came from some sort of professional glee . . . something to get your teeth into. Talk it over at a conference . . . 'well, Henry, I had one in Wandsworth, *what* a fruit cake . . . never seen nuffing like it, Henry . . . nutter? Nutter ain't in it. Turned over some poor old git on Bond Street, won't give old bill any account of himself except to say he's guilty and then he's slung down to me to try to find out what, if anything, Henry, is going on inside the old cranianianium. Competely round the twist, of course . . . doolally, you know? I found it in his marriage . . . yes, well it all comes down to sex doesn't it. Well, old chap, no need for shirtiness. Don't get like that. Stay off the pink gins at lunch time, there's my advice' (Henry wanders off. Cummings turns to his patient, who's desperately trying to wriggle out of a bottle of formaldehyde). 'Fucking miserable old bastard, Alfred, eh? Miserable miserable miserable. I'd have popped the cork and shown you to him if he hadn't been so miserable.'

'Well I've decided mate that it's a load of crap and it's not going any further. I'm cutting out. Go shrink someone else . . . sir.' Elf smiled for the 'sir'. He'd enjoyed that.

'We've been through all that, Hicks. That's not the situation.' Cummings' voice trailed off. He tapped his biro on the edge of the desk. He had interviewed this man twice before, and, even leaving the matter of the eye aside, Michael Cummings could see a marked deterioration in Hicks' physique. He watched his patient, surprised now as much by his ability to concentrate as by what he saw. The complexion was pasty, the hair was greasy with no sheen. Hicks' gestures appeared awkward, executed hastily. He looked like a maltreated dog.

'I've heard from me wife sir.' Elf volunteered.

Cummings nodded.

'Go on.'

'She says she wants out of it. D'you want to talk about her now?'

Cummings had continued to nod slowly and thoughtfully as he wrote. We all get women that want their way out, Hicks.

'Do you mind that?'

'No sir. I don't care hardly. We'd split long since, so. If this hadn't happened she'd have had a divorce off me anyway.'

'This?'

'What I'm doing bird for, sir. The dirty deed. The geezer I done. *Killed*. That's what you wanted me to say, isn't it? You've sat there for a couple of weeks waiting for that, haven't you?'

'I'm not in command of what you should or shouldn't say. I'd prefer you to speak honestly, I'd prefer if you didn't use bad language, but I'm not taking responsibility for you. You must say what's in your mind.'

'And how would I know that? . . .' Elf waved his hand impatiently at Cummings. 'No . . . no, don't worry about that. I've admitted to the police that I topped that geezer . . . killed him. I've said it in court . . . "Guilty, sir". I admit it to myself. *I did it* . . . topped him right out. I did it . . . I topped him. I'm using the word here, with you. Killed. I am contrite. Do you understand? Am I *clear* to you sir?'

Cummings sat unmoved. He half expected Elf to go on but this didn't happen so after a while he said, 'Yes, you're clear,' as a prod.

Elf shook his head violently,

'I'm not clear to you mate. Never. That's your mistake. You can't understand me because there's no way to, not unless you'd been *me*, and even then not to say for sure . . . what can you know about me, sir, all your degrees and everything? Don't answer, I know that's not the deal. You know what the answer is.'

'I'm not here to defend myself to you.' Cummings would have gone on but Elf slapped his hands on his thighs and stood.

'You can guess but you can't *know*. Even I'm not sure what my life is, how or why I do things . . . how can you know?'

Michael Cummings could see the screw's eye at the spyhole. He didn't want to call him in.

'Sit down. *Do*.'

Elf would not sit for a second. His ribs ached like all hell from last night's disagreement with his cellmate and he'd forgotten until he slammed the hands on his thighs. Now this pain had caught him up and he clutched under his armpit and winced. He sat down gently.

'No one knows. Not even you. *Think* about it . . . *sir*.' Elf leaned forward on the desk, careful not to move his left arm quickly again and disturb the bruised ribs. 'You might be the cleverest bloke in the world and come out with all sorts of theories, but if the place you started from was wrong, you've duffed it . . . sir.'

Elf stood again, noticing that there was a whole shelf full of *Wisdens* in the corner of the room. Noticing that this room and this man were the most pleasant things in the whole place. More pleasant even than the library. More pleasant than being a trusty in the screws' bar and canteen, that's what everyone wants here, they all reckon it's that pleasant. But talking to a man who gets some of what you're babbling on about is probably even more pleasant than that.

'I'm sorry, sir. It's hard to concentrate. Can we finish?'

Elf sat down again, still looking at the books he believed were *Wisdens*. He leaned back in the chair, letting his head ease back and closing his eyes. He was very tired. He'd been tired for weeks and weeks. Weeks. Elf had given his name dozens of times to dozens of officials. He'd given his age dozens of times and his 'marital status' dozens of times. Perhaps hundreds of times, Elf couldn't remember. He didn't want to. He'd talked to policemen, lawyers, more policemen (who'd accused him of the most exotic crimes in an attempt to improve the rate at which they solved exotic crimes), more lawyers, a social worker or two. He'd once talked to Carol when she'd visited. He'd *had* to do all the talking then, all she could do was cry. Elf had talked to cellmates (until this newest), to old men who were in for dishonest handling or gaining pecuniary advantage by deception (now *there*'s a crime that could do with a wider audience) and sat playing chess next to him during 'association periods' and squeezed along their bench a little when he told them what he was in for. Elf had even talked to the man he shared a cell with now and was bigger than Elf and felt entitled to give his desires full rein once the cell door slammed. If he starts them tricks again I'll give him a right seeing to, don't matter how big he is. Everyone talks and everyone asks the wrong question. They say 'why'. Why?

Elf looked up at the dozen or so *Wisdens*. Why? Why anything? It's so bloody naïve. Why should a trick-cyclist have *Wisdens* in the jug?

'How do you feel Hicks?' Blunt instrument, medicine.

Elf's chair creaked. 'More tea, vicar?'

'Just concentrate on what's happening here. A lot of people will want some sort of answer. How do you feel about the incident?'

Elf shook his head. He could visualize Cummings with his fellow do-gooders in this room, state-paid do-gooders gathered round to pick over the bones of his psyche. 'What *I* can't understand is his lack of demonstration. He *says* he is contrite . . . but he doesn't demonstrate it'; Elf could see the Assistant Governor, the M.O., Cummings and some welfare worker all nodding like a group of oriental sages, yes yes, he doesn't look as if his feelings are real. He's a very evil and cunning man, yes yes (all nod again). Gives no real sign, yes yes, well I reckon we ought to sling the key away, yes yes, right. That's him pigeon-holed then. Who's next?

'Well?' Cummings asked again.

'Well what?'

'How do you feel? How do you feel about the man's death, how do you feel about the prospect of staying in a place like this for a long time? It's what people will want to know if they're to make any sort of decision over you.'

Elf shook his head again.

'What people?'

Michael Cummings pushed the button. He had his own problems and wasn't about to get philosophical with an inmate. He was tired enough as it was. Get rid of Hicks and go home.

Elf walked down the drab corridors in front of his pet screw. He'd leant the rules about this, and stood clear of the door so that he presented no threat to the prison officer or to the man's colleague who would open the door. He guessed they were apprehensive lest he leap up and sink his fangs into the back of their blue shirted necks. Elf had learnt to keep his prison clothes and his cell neat and tidy, which is what they all like round here. He'd learned his way around, I know my way round. He'd even kept his mouth shut when he'd fought (and lost) with the big ape last night. 'Fell over, sir.'

Everyone has a question. Elf walked in front of the screw, boots of both men clipping and clanging on the metal catwalk. Everyone has a question, screw, what's yours?

'Wait there boy.'

'Yes sir.' Elf waited. He knew. He knew he'd had a dream

where a young man, it may have been himself, descends to a tiled and crowded place (it may have been a tube station) and the young man is almost delirious and doesn't know it. He knew the man in the dream had rested well once in his own flat and dreamt about taking revenge for an awful thing that had been done to his friend, and he'd got up sweating, for fear and for anger, swabbing his neck with a damp towel in the bathroom and coming into the living-room to sit upon the cheap old (new) furniture that would make your neck ache if you sat still for too long.

The young man had sat still for a very long time, sometimes running his hands nervously through his hair while he puzzled over the dream . . . yes, the dream. To find the man responsible and take revenge. He looked at his hands. Was it in them to do this? But the dream had been so vivid. It was so right. Would I have the nerve for that? He thought probably not. It was a very quiet night and there was a soft patter of rain at the window. The young man pulled the curtains apart for a second to see, then allowed them to fall. And the interviews in the dream, they'd seemed so real. And that man. The blue eyes and finely creased skin, oh I must have known him from somewhere. I must have done. And the institutional smells, I can smell them now even! He sniffed slightly, then smiled at his own stupidity. It's such a silly idea. He went to the bedroom to check the clock . . . three.

The young man pulled on some clothes, jeans, a shirt, a thick donkey jacket. He kissed his wife gently and she moaned the way people do at three a.m. when they're either in the arms of a dream lover or they can smell the beautiful dinner you'll take them to tomorrow night, all dressed up in a monkey suit, darling. She moaned again but didn't hear the click of the lock as he left. She wasn't there. Elf knew the young man was kissing a mirage within his dream.

The first growls of buses and lorries from a winter morning find him walking by the side of a canal, a cement-made path recently built. There's a scrapyard opposite and he can pick out, in the street lights, the half dismembered fifties lorries, the ones with the big bull-nose and split windscreen, great hulks of red metal, he can't see them shrivelling with each rainfall, but they do. All of it patrolled by a half-starved alsatian who'd be frightened and vicious at one and the same time.

The young man in Elf's dream was pleased there was a canal's width at least between him and the scrapyard dog. There had been attempts to clean up the canalside, but it was hard to say whether it had worked or not. The steps down from the street were better built now, and there was mosaics on the wall. The canal was full of rubbish, the young man knew though he couldn't see, just a black ink strip stretched before him, flashing and stinging light if you looked along rather than in it, varnished. He turned and made his way to the steps, climbing quickly to the street, ignoring the dog this time. He went to an all-night coffee stall. It was surrounded by gentlemen of the road in various stages of decay. They had broken some pallets from Spitalfields and built a fire. Now the gentlemen of the road were gathered around the flames, and the steam from their breath and the yellow light of their fire made them look an otherworldly group, misshapen bodies hidden by the shadow . . . not threatening, no evil or malice, none of that, no. Just depressed from the main flow of life, men whose spirits had been hidden and now, touched by the fire's light, were revealed. Men such as us, thought the young man moving through Elf's dream, and then he recoiled, since he had strayed too near to the men of the road and smelled them.

He drank. The coffee was bitter. The young man was not, or so he thought. He was just working his head out.

Elf lay on the bunk and purposefully put aside the young man and the dream. He thought about a young woman who'd be sitting in a bedsit and with any luck wouldn't be thinking about him. He hoped not. Elf thought about another place, another continent, and another woman there. It was just as well she wasn't around . . . what a mess! He hoped both young women wouldn't be thinking of him, sort of return post.

He could deal with all this, this 'yessir' and 'nosir', 'keep your mouth shut'. He'd have to deal with it for a long time but Elf believed he could, given the concentration. He'd *have* to. He'd pay attention to the rules and keep his mouth shut. He should take that psychiatrist more seriously though, he knew, otherwise he'd end up in the funny farm full of some sedative, dribbling down the front of his straitjacket and not knowing what day it was.

Elf wondered about a Detective Inspector who'd kept quiet when he'd been nicked. Very wise, that, or maybe he didn't know. Hardly, though. A D.I. would hardly be likely to miss that. Elf turned to the dream again. He rested fully on the bunk, placing his flat palms behind his head and wriggling a little for comfort, or rather to accommodate the discomfort in his rib-cage. Elf wondered if he'd be able to whistle up the dream again tonight. There seemed so much to do in it, as if he could live through dreaming, moving through his prison-sleep life during the day and only going out at night, when he dreamed. That'd be a good plan. They think I'm locked up but I can dream out any time I want.

He could hear the prison sounds reflected through the walls, distant work sounds that he'd escaped because of his visit to the psychiatrist. They wouldn't finish work for another three-quarters of an hour and that time was his. He would try to dream up his doppelganger. If he could do it as and when he wanted he would live and breath through that.

No. Elf sat up suddenly, ribs hurting but he let it hurt. He swung his feet to the floor and let it hurt again. He picked up a paperback novel from the little table he shared with his cell-mate and began to read. He couldn't concentrate. Elf tossed the book the length of the bunk.

'Guderian was a panzer general,' he smiled. 'Guderian was a panzer bleeding general.'

He stood and walked to the barred window. He could see plenty of sky but that was all. Some small hawk, Elf couldn't see exactly which, was hovering, then wheeling and diving, then climbing to hover again, all short dives, as if it were after fun, or hadn't made up its mind yet. The bird wheeled one last time and dived quickly from sight, staying down this time.

Elf turned on his heel, wheeling also from the window, and sat down to begin his time.